Alan & Lotte Marcus Legacy Series #1
in celebration of 64-years of a soulmate marriage

Incident in Fargos County

ALAN MARCUS

Alan and Lotte Marcus Legacy Series #1

Incident in Fargos County

ISBN-13: 978-0-9629909-2-2

Other Shores Press. Carmel, CA
Copyright © 2019 by Lotte Marcus

Lotte Marcus
95 Corona Way
Carmel, CA 93923
lottedoc@prodigy.net

"Very good, remarkable... In fact, I have
As high an opinion of this talent, as anything
I have encountered in a long while..."

——Saul Bellow

Author's Note

"Incident in Fargos Country" was originally written over sixty years ago with the expressed intent of a movie sale in mind. In those days I found myself rather unexpectedly, living in film land --- result of my wining a prestigious literary prize sponsored by both *The Atlantic Monthly* magazine and *MGM* studios which carried with it --- among other rewards --- a free trip to the West Coast and a possible job offer as a screenwriter. Being a freelance by choice and temperament, however, I soon found a way to make strategic raids on Hollywood's substantial financial assets, -- enough to pay for groceries for my growing family and to subsidize as well my incorrigible addiction to the beguilements of prose fiction – an addiction I shamelessly admit – even in this present era of digitalized Steve Jobs-sian text, click, and "share" rituals – I'm *still* indelibly fixated on, in the effort to discover the kind of truths, which only literature, in my view, -- and particularly the novel, -- *"the mirror in the roadway"* – as Balzac called it, -- is ultimately capable of revealing to us.

Like so many movie-goers, though – I was – am—a confirmed Western buff. Which is why I began foraging for promising movie material, by looking at the bitter conflicts that used to rage between Sheep Herders and Cattle Men in the 1800s out on the Nebraska, Wyoming. and Arizona plains, a conflict known to history books as the Johnson County Wars. But since I was also a huge admirer of William Faulkner's small-scale masterpiece "As I Lay Dying," I decided to try to use it as a model for the story I had in mind to tell, -- to *mimic*, if I could, the novel's wonderful, intricate, and sui generis "architecture." During the subsequent writing, however, something unexpected happened: -- the manuscript abruptly began to blossom under my fingers into one of the most phenomenal writing experiences of my entire career!

In a word, writing this tale simply soon took me by storm; I remember, each day, I'd go to bed exhausted but always wake up the next morning, raring to go… The form itself--borrowed from the Faulknerian original,-- amounted to a kind of revolving stage structure; i.e. successive characters each taking over the first person narration for a few pages, (like runners in a relay race passing the baton from one to another.) That is, whoever happened to be doing the speaking, would hold the spotlight for a few pages, -- projecting his or her own voice, tone, temperament, predicament etc. until the *next* narrator, with another voice, temperament, rhythm, and persona would take over. The trick was to keep the "larger" plot simultaneously moving forward at the same time as the revolving monologues – i.e. – disclosing what happened when a loosely knit band of hired mercenaries, -- a ragtag informal would-be militia – tried to lay siege to the holdings and fertile fields of a lone sheep farmer, working his own ranch by himself in an obscure corner of the Arizona plains.

Writing this story – turned into an unprecedented writing adventure unique in my entire career… Only a week into it and I felt myself becoming virtually "airborne". The characters on their revolving stages, seem to keep returning faster and faster, the complications and voices kept intermingling in an increasing tempo of fear, astonishment, courage, greed, revolt., Until at the end, resolution (and redemption), ---- (under my struggling –to-keep-up-fingers) --- fell perfectly into place!

"Incident in Fargos County," is one of those "miracles", which – if one is lucky, one may be vouchsafed perhaps once or twice, during a writing lifetime. Over the years, many of my friends who read "Fargos" – and admired it, -- kept wondering why I didn't try putting it out into the world by itself, as a stand-alone "read." I'm afraid I never had a good answer for them --- I always seemed to be too busy somehow doing something else… Besides. so far as I was concerned, - it had already achieved its main purpose --- it was bought quickly by MGM and subsequently turned into a kind of cult Western under another title ("The Marauders") though my then agent was initially aghast at the "form" I'd chosen to submit it in – he was convinced it was too "complicated", as written, to ever reach pay dirt.. I myself, -- after finishing it, didn't want to have anything to do with its movie version since I instinctively knew that coping with the unavoidable group-think" filter of a major studio production, would inevitably bring with it the kind of let-down – that I simply didn't want – after the trancelike- euphoria of its lightning bolt-like composition – to undergo…

Through the years, however, I've sneakily toyed with a secret urge to put this favorite personal piece of mine, -- my Faulknerian –"clone", as it were, -- between covers. And – hallelujah! – I'm really happy to see that this is finally coming to pass!

AM

(Marcus Legacy Archives){1}

Dedication

This book is dedicated to two novels by two wonderful writers which, over the years, have been a continuing source of pleasure, inspiration, and example to me.

The first, is William Faulkner's *"As I Lay Dying"* (published in 1930) which Prof Harold Bloom, Sterling Prof of Humanities at Yale, & ceaseless advocate of the best in our native literature, - has called his most original novel, -,part of that astonishing string of masterpieces the novelist produced during his most productive decade, 1930-1939, (for which he eventually received the Nobel Prize.)

As already noted in the Author's Note-----Faulkner's 48 "revolving first-person monologues in *Dying"*-twelve more than the 36 I created in *"Fargos County"*—invented a brilliantly original way of combining event and character, such that each acts as a continual "catalyst" upon the other…The central tale------the drama of one clan of isolated Mississippi back country folk struggling to come to terms with the dying of their bed-ridden burnt-out matriarch, has them eventually transporting the old woman's corpse in a home-built coffin through a gauntlet of fire, flood and caved-in bridges, on a rickety mules-pulled wagon to her original kin's burying grounds. But the trajectory of the narrative itself is constantly being skewered and altered by the echo chamber effect of the monologues themselves, ---a revolving cataract of voices, invoking quarrels *un*resolved, promises never kept, recriminations still unforgiven, hidden hopes and furtive dreams still clung to; indeed, the effect of this revolving testimony amounts to bravura (non-chronological) glimpses into rural Southern life, expressed in pure distilled Mississippi dialect, like a series of smuggled communiques handed-down from a non-stop (& multi-generational) domestic civil war…To me, the unsolvable mystery of this novel is how such an erstwhile "primitive" "country", saga, ends up ---through the sheer artistry of the author's inimitable style--as a kind of deliberately encoded

ix

meditation about what used to called the " *Human Condition*"..---
Precisely how Faulkner pulls this astounding feat off, I still
haven't---after God knows how many *re*readings--- figured
out…But each time I pick up *"Dying"*, I usually see something in
it I hadn't seen before…"

The second novel I want to cite is Walter Van Tilburg Clark's
":The Oxbow Incident", a mesmerizing anatomy of an imagined
Western lynching., first published in 1940. To this day *"Ox Bow"*,
in my view, because of its simplicity of style, subtlety of
characterization, and depth of vision---stands head and shoulders
above the multitude of similar tales featuring far less differentiated
frontier types focused on the same time and place. Here I have to
agree with Clifton Fadiman, a distinguished book critic of the 40's
decade, who declared Ox Bow stands in the same relationship to an
ordinary Western as the *"Maltese Falcon"* does to an ordinary
detective story." He goes on to add, **"I think it's what we'd have
to call a masterpiece.."**

I enthusiastically concur. But let me add that—beneath its
western veneer---"Ox Bow" is essentially the exploration of a moral
conundrum: how can the idea of a free society, one passionately
concerned –ostensibly—with liberty, equality, and the democratic
administration of "justice"—as envisioned by our founding fathers
with their far-sighted system of checks and balances eloquently
embedded in the Constitution—be reconciled with—or even be fitfully
tolerant of—the sporadically threatening ----and plainly subversive—
eruptions against (and open contempt for)—various institutional
safeguards erected to protect the rule of law and, indeed, the integrity
of civil society itself, which all school children are taught to revere in
our classrooms? Whether we're looking back to pre-Nation Salem
witch burning days or up through the centuries, we still find ourselves
confronting periodic assaults upon lawfully laid-down---and
legislatively approved—measures to ventilate--& debate—dissent
from unpopular policies. And the same anti-democratic inclinations
have kept continuously asserting themselves across the years, spawned
partly by the contaminating legacy of the African Slave Trade itself,
which led to the shameful blight of Jim Crow, the Klu Klux clan cross
burnings &--ultimately—our blood soaked Civil War; then later, came

the Ruby Ridge shootout, the Branch Dividians tragedy, Timothy McVeith and the Oklahoma City bombing, and the rash of xenophobic, conspiratorial militias, like the Posse Comitatus etc.. In recent times— we've witnessed the behavior of bullying Tea Party thugs trying to intimidate peaceful democratic town hall meetings discussing Obamacare in the summer of 2009, brazenly shouting plainly out-of-context lines hijacked from Thomas Jefferson *"The Tree of Liberty"* they chanted (from their obviously pre-rehearsed script!)) *"must be periodically watered by the blood of tyrants!"*

As a nation, we're still trying--though often *failing* – to contain or curb that infamous paranoid tendency on the part of disaffected fellow-citizens, tempted by the lure of vengeful action to take the law into their *own* hands, -- heedlessly trashing the Constitution while yielding to that mindlessness which scapegoat-seeking always engenders, making them prime candidates for the catharsis of vigilante-ism itself—(and its pathology which is inevitably mob-driven!) – something mirrored unforgettably in *"Ox Bow"* and dramatized yet again, I'm proud to say, in *"Incident In Fargos Country"*

AM

CONTENTS

PRELUDE

It just goes to show you, you never know! Because if
I'd a rode South like I was going to with Sanchez and the
rest of his boys, I would've left Dallas a week before the
Colonel showed up, would've missed the best deal of my
life so far! Talk about setups – here we are aboard this
regular private train rolling toward the border of Arizona at
sixty miles an hour, with all we can eat and drink, two
hundred bucks a piece guaranteed, bullets enough to blow
up Cheyenne, and twenty dollars extra for every rustler
killed in Fargo's county!

Why it's just like the Colonel promised when he
recruited us back in Dallas, him with his old Civil War
uniform on and all those medals shining like a tray full of
junk jewelry.

"New horses for each man," he told us. "Brand new
Pintos. And after we reach Buffalo, they're yours to ride
away with."

"Who's paying for this little expedition?" someone
asked.

"You fixing to join the Corps?"

"Corps, what Corps?"

2

"That's what I'm recruiting for," he said. "A Corps of avengers, men. We aim to teach those Washington politicians a few lessons. All those miserable sheep kissing speechmakers pass a few laws, and think they can take away what our fathers earned by blood and bullets, as if these plains were free to every cussed brand stealer east of the Rockies who thinks he can come in here and settle down and take away our fundamental rights."

"Ain't those public lands open to settlement?" somebody asked. That set him off again. He's the goddamdest man for making speeches.

"Free to settlement!" he yelled. "And what are we supposed to do meanwhile – sit around and watch while a bunch of sneaking miserable cattle thieves comes in and rustles our stock and takes away fodder land we give our sons up for, fattening themselves up at our expense? Oh they're a pestilence, men," he yelled. "A miserable pestilence, and we got to act now, we got to make them think twice before deciding to bring their cussed wagons and sheep and God only knows what else out here cutting our acreage out from under us, ruining our plains just because the damn politicians pass a law saying it's legal."

"So what I'm calling for is volunteers," he went on. "There's two hundred dollars apiece in it for whoever's

3

willing to ride herd on a miserable list of cattle thieves in Fargos County. Who'll step forward and help us show 'em we still aim to say what's done with our own land?"

No one moved an inch. We just kept staring at him. Because he wasn't fooling us none, he only come down to Texas because he couldn't get enough men back home up in Wyoming or Arizona. Probably afraid they'd be recognized. And we still didn't know who was putting the money out for this Colonel to play crusader with.

Still, two hundred dollars is two hundred dollars.

"I reckon I'll take a chance," I finally said. I saw him looking at the hook where my right hand should have been. "Grab hold for a bargain" I said, holding the hook out.

Right then I seen what this Colonel was made of! Like a coon dog, lots of noise and bluster, but inside, butter where his blood should have been!. Because he didn't say a thing to me, didn't even ask me how come I wanted to ride herd with hardware instead of a right hand. No, he didn't even get mad at that hook held up instead of fingers.

So right away I began to see all kinds of possibilities.

"Come on, men," I yelled, lathering up those Dallas boys standing around in a wondering circle. "That two

4

hundred is only to begin with," And half of that two
hundred's in advance, isn't that right Colonel?"

"Why..," he began. He looked at me sort of puzzled.
But I went right on taking it away from him. "Yes sir," I told
them, appointing myself his deputy without anyone's asking
a by-your-leave. "One hundred right in your pocket. And
we're not forgetting the pony,- that's another fifty dollars
clear! And all for a few days work, only did I say *work*? Since
when's riding herd on rustlers work for any Texan?" I yelled.

It took some talking but finally they began signing up.
Eventually around twenty put their names down. And all the
time, the Colonel, he looked like he didn't know whether to
thank me or shoot me...

Well, he still don't know yet. And here we are on this
train they had waiting on the yards outside of town, and
something's going to happen soon. I'm not worried about
the money, this train took more'n hot air to outfit, didn't it?
But still, so far, all we're getting is speeches by the Colonel.
Like right now we're sitting around again, his medals shining
in our faces, his wheezy voice going on some more, all
about "the glorious spirit of our great tradition, etc., etc.,."
Everyone's drinking like at a goddam banquet. "Who was it
first tamed this country?" cries the Colonel, "planted roots
here, showed what guts and fortitude could do?"   How

5

about some cash in advance?" someone yells from the table.

Everything grows still. And I can tell we've been drinking too much, though the Colonel sounds just the same, whether you're liquored up or not. "We've been listening to you sound off a half a day," someone says. (It's Big Joe Ramos from South of Dallas.) "How about showing us the color of some currency for a change?" he goes on.

The Colonel draws himself up. Looks at me. Clears his throat. Outside the window, it's dark now, and there isn't anything to be seen, just grazing land underneath stars, and us moving so slow you might think the locomotive was straining on a hill, instead of crawling in the middle of Arizona prairie land.

"How do we know the whole thing aint a wild goose chase?" yells Joe Ramos, and those other Texans don't say a word. Liquor's apt to make 'em ugly. "Us out here in the middle of nowhere, and so far we haven't seen a nickel change hands!" shouts Ramos.

"Wait a minute boys," I tell them. "You heard what the colonel explained. We got to get to Rendezvous Point."

"Rendezvous Point, what Rendezvous Point?"

"Why you heard the way the Colonel explained it..."I begin...

Just then the train gives a bump and a kind of screech and comes to a dead stop. It's pitch black outside. So there we are, hundreds of miles away from Cheyenne, with a train full of ammunition and a big cache of water and food supplies and various other emergency equipment and repair stuff and those prairie wolves howling beyond the windows and no lights to be seen, nothing anywhere, and our engine deader'n a coyote's corpse.

"Gentlemen," says the Colonel, rising, "I think we've arrived."

PERCY KETTERING

What faces, what amazing faces! Oh I only hope I brought enough sketch pads along. Such real Western types these are, and even Roy looks different, saddled and holstered as he is. But I have to keep pinching myself to believe it's really true! Because when Roy asked me to come out with him, naturally I jumped at the chance, how many Englishmen have ever seen the American West? Oh and when I think how Roy used to walk around at school, so quiet and restrained, hardly anyone really believed that talk about a big ranch and hundreds of acres of range land, and thousands of head of cattle. But my word, it's even more fantastic than he said. Because look at us, here we are now, not only Roy senior and junior but all this equipment and wagons and horses, and waiting in the middle of the plain for a signal light to be flashed miles away from a stopped trainful of Texans. Why, it's something straight out of Fenimore Cooper. They'll never believe me back in Devonshire.

Oh, oh. Flash. The light just winked on. Yes, that'll mean they already arrived at Rendezvous Point. There's Roy's father giving us the signal to ride forward. So now I'll have to try and hold on again, whoever said learning to ride would be easy, my seat's already a raw wound. Ow. Blast this bloody beast!. Ouch. I better think of something to take my mind off. Well perhaps I might write this whole thing up for one of the London dailies, make a bit of a splash, what! Simple Justice On The American Frontier – something like that? Yes, and how would it go on from there? … *When increasing thievery and vandalism plagued the cattlemen of Fargos county, Arizona, last year, at least two hardy frontiersmen didn't bother to wait for legislatures and lawmakers. Squire Roy L. Rutherford, owner of ten thousand acres in South Fargos county, personally rallied his own private forces under the command of Colonel Julian B. Samson, also a local cattle raiser, and together these two men recruited a band of liberty loving frontiersmen*

8

dedicated to the arrest and chastisement of a group of outlaw homesteaders who for twelve months past had been terrorizing..."

Hello, we're stopped. What's happening? Is that the Colonel himself getting off the train? Yes, my word, it must be, look at that chest full of medals. But something's wrong, the Squire and he seem to be having words. If I can only nudge this balky animal a little closer...

"None at all?" the Colonel says. "But you promised me at least fifteen more from local sources."

And the Squire: "They just wouldn't join. Someone's told them they're liable to be reprised against. They've got families living hereabouts."

And the Colonel: "I've only got twenty Texans aboard."

"That ought to still be plenty for what we planned," says the Squire. "Roy's going along too, and I'm sending Ridgley to look after the stores. And that Englishman that's here from school with Roy, he wants to draw pictures of what we're doing."

"Pictures?" says the Colonel, brightening up considerably, "Picture of me?"

So after the tents are set for the night, and everyone has eaten, and the train has left, with the Squire on it after

9

having made a rather rousing lecture to the men about driving the bandits back where they came from, the Colonel comes and sits for me by candlelight. A big man, face like burned mutton. Arms moving back and forth, voice rumbling. Talking about the Civil War, something about the strategy of the Large Attack. Wonderful native American type, real heroic caste to him.

But all at once the tent flap moves again. In comes Mr. Roy Junior, together with his clerk Ridgley, and my word, who is that chap with them? A saturnine face, chin bone scarred, and with a hook instead of a right hand. Yes, I swear it, a regular hook!

"Colonel," says Roy Junior "Did you promise these men half their fee in advance?"

"Well, as a matter of fact, Sir..." The Colonel begins...

"And the rest where we get to Buffalo, Sir" interrupts Mr. Hook himself in a queer type of drawl I've never heard before. "According to our agreement, Sir."

"But you know we won't be able to pay anything out of banks in Buffalo," says Roy Junior. "Not after what will have transpired by then. And as for that hundred you're taking about in advance..."

"Begging your pardon, Sir," says Mr. Hook with a grin of pure obsequiousness, warped under candlelight, "your

10

figures want straightening a little. That's *a hundred and fifty in advance, Sir."* he says.

"A hundred and fifty !"

"We aint used to acting as stevedores," he says. "Which is what we've been doing for the past two hours here, I believe, though I don't recollect anything was said to that effect in the contract."

"By God, you..."

"Fair is fair, with all due respect, Sir," the Hook says, grinning once again.

Oh these rugged American ranchers with their simple codes! Yes, even in negotiation, everything's so frank, open, unconcealed. That's what we need back home,– a little more of their noble simplicity of spirit, their disarming willingness to face facts.

Well I must write all about it in my article.

ROY, JR.

Half the day gone, and only these few miles traveled! I don't like it. We should've got to Smith's place by now at least. Well, if Father hadn't had to ride back to Claremont for gold to pay these men off with... stupid wranglers, where

11

do they think they're going to spend it? And now here's the front wagon axle partially cracked, on top of everything else. But the Colonel doesn't seem to mind. "Good place to draw our battle plan," he says. Battle plan?– What kind of a damn battle plan do we need! We have the list of names, don't we? So just ride in, burn'em out, string 'em up! Let everyone see we mean it this time – no more Eastern poachers hiding behind an Act of Congress, coming out here and ruining good cattle graze with their sheep, and their orneriness, and their air of owning everything in sight. Range land belongs to those who claimed it first, don't it? Well, they'll find out what we mean.

Oh, Christ. Here comes Father's clerk, Ridgley, again, with a watchdog look in his eye. I swear I never saw a more sneaky busy-body of a man.

"Mr. Roy," he says. "Are you going to tell the Colonel to take his uniform off?"

"Why, goddam it, Ridgley?"

"Rider's coming from the North," he says. "Won't do to have him see what we're aiming at. If we're supposed to be a peaceful party of "*surveyors...*"

12

"But I don't see how—"

"Men are getting restless, too, Mr. Roy," he says. "It's hot out here on this plain. How long you figure the Colonel's going to be mapping out his strategy?"

"Goddam it, Ridgley, how should I know?"

"Another thing, he promised 'em all a pony," says Ridgley. "The one they call Hook was just speaking to me about it. We've only got eighteen Pintos, and two of them Texans is riding the wagon. So do I pay the difference?"

"What am I, the Commander here? Why not ask the Colonel?"

"Your Pa said you was to be considered in charge, Mr. Roy. And if you don't mind, there's something else..."

"Now what is it, for Chrissakes?"

"Your friend, Mr. Kettering. Look at him, there he is, sitting over there, drawing us while we're talking! He's already made half a dozen pictures of the men's faces. This little party isn't exactly legal,Sir. And if those pictures were to get into certain hands..."

"He'll draw any goddam face he wants!" I shout. "He's a friend of mine, that's what he came out West for,-- to draw the Arizona country. Why he doesn't even know what this is all about, Ridgley -- to him we're some kind of vigilantes on a regular citizen's crusade. So let him draw anything he wants and keep your snoopy face out of it!"

That spying Ridgley! I swear I'll have it out with him ,once and for all, one of these days! Always snooping and snooping around – he ought to be checking up on sticky-fingered customers in a store somewhere! And what'd he come out West for in the first place? We never did really find out! His health, he said once. But how do we know he wasn't lying? Well I don't see why the old man wanted to hire him to begin with.

Still, he's right about one thing– the Colonel's uniform, and it's up to me to mention it. So I go over to where the old man is sitting, pouring over his maps. But soon's I tell him, he rears back, furious.

"Take it off?" he yells. "As if I was ashamed of it. My old uniform...?"

"It's only till that rider passes, Colonel..."

"Surveyor or not, I've got a right to wear this uniform!"

"I don't like to order you, Colonel..."

"*You* order *me*?," he says. "Aren't you a little mixed up, son? Trying to contravene the chain of command...?"

"Command be damned!..."

But as it turns out, who should come riding up but Sheriff Angus of nearby Claremont county, the same man

14

who helped the Squire out last year in a little matter of securing water rights. Maybe he even contributed a little *himself* when father went polling ranchers last week for help with this little party's cash flow problem..

"*Surveying party*." he says, winking. "Oh sure. Land needs to be "*surveyed*" real bad, I hear. Well, you got yourself a right nice group of "*surveyors*" by the looks of things," he says, giving us a long stare...

But finally we start moving again, those Texans squabbling all the while about who was to ride horse and who wagon, and that noon sun blazing down, and sweat pouring off everybody in buckets, and the Colonel stopping here and there, to reconnoiter, as he says. Dust keeps bothering our eyes, and nothing to cool our tempers. But finally we come to the first troublemakers place, a fellow by the name of Abner Smith.

But when we pull up close, all we can do is sit amazed, staring.

"What is it," asks Percy. "Fire?"

Fire hell! All around the yard's full of cinders and rubbish and what's left of Smith and his wife buried under that debris of cabin and dead sheep. Then Ramos, one of the Texans, bends down and picks up a small piece of

15

metal, about a few inches long. Comanche Arrowhead. At that, everybody begins craning necks in all directions.

"Why we're in luck," I tell them. "Because they just saved us some work here is all. Indians haven't been seen in this country for months, so it was probably some wandering strays from north Cheyenne. The sheriff didn't mention it, he'd know if they were acting up again, wouldn't he? So all we got is one less to worry about," I tell them, crossing Smith's name off the list, trying to make it seem like nothing.

But the Texans aren't too happy now, what with that place smelling like it does, and Smith's body already turning cold, and the hill country right in front of us, perfect for ambush. No one moves at all for a few seconds. And when we finally turn North again here are two Dallas boys already deciding the scenery's not apt to be to their liking. Throw their gold pieces right on the ground, ride off straight South on two of the old man's new Pintos, don't say a word.

Ridgley's the only one who gets excited. "Rank thievery!" he yells. "Are you going to let them get away with it, Mr. Roy?"

"Shut up, Ridgley."

"But you'll never see those horses again!" he shouts. Your father paid good money for'em, and put me in charge to see..."

"Are you going to shut up?"

The Colonel's riding with his mouth half open, like he's not sure whether to say something to us or not. Hot sun overhead, tempers sore, all of us moving slowly due north, deeper into hill country. And suddenly here's that one with the hook hand (Blanding's his name) riding alongside, whispering something confidential into my ear.

"Not that I want to make trouble," he says, "but look at the added risk we're taking, Mr. Roy. So how about if we split up what those two other boys turned back amongst ourselves? Because we didn't figure on Indian fighting." he says. "That changes the picture now, don't it?"

"My father paid you once, Blanding. If you don't like the arrangement..."

"Fair is fair, Mr. Roy," he says.

I reign up. Everybody's looking at us. The Colonel's eyes are on me, and I can feel him sort of wavering.

"Straight South and take the third fork," I say. "Ride hard enough, you might even make Claremont before sundown."

17

"Why Mr. Roy," Blanding cries. (He has a whiney voice sometimes, but his eyes are regular cougar eyes) "You think I'm the kind of man that'd desert just because of a little disagreement?" he says. "Comanches about, and us out here in the middle of the wilderness? Why I'm downright surprised at you, Mr. Roy!." he says.

His face grins. But I keep watching his gun left hand. No one says anything for a few seconds, and then the Colonel orders us both to quit arguing, get back to the trail.

"Yes Sir, Colonel," cries Blanding. "Because after all, it's you who're commanding us now, isn't it Sir?" he says.

I don't say a word. Just keep my eyes glued to his gun hand.

RIDGLEY

If it weren't for the fact that he's Mr. Roy's son, I wouldn't let him get away with it,- yelling at me like that in front of these men! Who'll protect his father's interests if I don't – not that decrepit fool of a Colonel, where did he ever get those medals? Civil War, he says. In a Crowfoot's eye! But I know what I got to do- keep my eyes wide open, period! . "Third in the chain of command" – that's what the

18

Squire told me. "I'm depending on you, Ridgley," he said. And he can, he can! Oh Jehovah, if I were only in charge of these mercenaries... look at them, all bunched together like that, one fusillade and where'd we be? But what's the use of mentioning it, all that young fool can do is yell at me. Well, he won't keep on doing it. I'll take just so much, son or no son! And if it comes to bullets, they have a surprise coming. All those nights practice shooting beyond the cistern – poor Ridgley shooting at the moon again, they used to laugh! Well, they'll see soon enough. No, they won't laugh if it comes to that...

Because I knew the old man was planning this little business long ago, who was it first set him on it? "Damn trouble makers," I used to tell him. "All these high and proud homesteaders, why pretty soon they'll be sharing water, building up herds to compete with yours. Sheep polluting your graze," I told him. "And water's not exactly abundant hereabouts. So master of all this acreage, or maybe one day bankrupt by troublemakers, take your pick," I said.

Because he just can't scare 'em! Raid their stock, try to buy 'em off, poison their feed – they still keep coming on! "You've got to protect yourself," I told the Squire. "And not just from brand stealers, though that's what a lot probably are, too,if you could prove it. But you've got to stop 'em from coming into the county so fast, because a few more years and it'll be not only cattle but *votes* as well."

Anyway, this is why I finally headed out West a long time ago and not just to add up figures!. Six months to live, the doctors told me back in Newark. But that was four years ago, back in '90, and wouldn't the bunch of them be surprised...

Doctors made my whole life wrong, so far, anyhow! Who was it kept me from the Military, certified my lungs as bad, if not doctors? But that was all damn foolishness – trying to stick somebody like me behind a desk, when I was cut out to be an outdoors type, maybe even a sea-fearing man, who knows...!

Well, two years of keeping the Squire's books and getting my strength back weren't wasted. Because here I am for a fact, third in command. "I'm giving you the flag." The Squire said. And said it to *me*, not to that peacock Colonel!... oh I know he's counting on me, and not only just to keep track of stores. *Discipline, Loyalty,*–I know what they mean! Don't worry, Squire. We'll string up those five troublemakers and march into Buffalo and hang this flag from the center of town as a warning. Then let anyone try to prove we weren't out just to kill cattle rustlers, let 'em try to prove it!... And that'll keep homesteaders from building up strength in these parts for a while. At least until we can get a new law fixed to limit public land sales. And by that time, we won't have to worry, things'll be consolidated by then. Sure, it's the Squire's strategy, he worked it out, but who put the idea in his head? Well, some day people'll know the truth!.

If only that colonel doesn't get us lost somewhere or give the whole thing away beforehand. And as for Mr. Roy, JR., he'd better watch his tongue! I'm not taking any more from him. Because these Texans aren't the best material for soldiers in the world, and suppose every officer got bawled out in front of his troops – where would discipline, loyalty, respect, go then?

After all, third in command is *still* third in command!.

COLONEL JULIAN B. SAMSON

"How long, Colonel?," asks young Mr. Roy.

"When my scouts get back," I tell him.

"But we can see from this hill. There is no one around for miles. And sun's going down. So why not ride in and flush that damn Everett out of there, and..."

"Don't get impatient, son. Don't pay to risk our necks for no reason.."

All these hot bloods – they're just plain ignorant of military strategy!. *Reconnoiter*, that's one rule you can't go wrong by! Always reconnoiter, search out the land!. Look at the way those two Texans are riding across that field – making perfect targets, sitting straight up! I told them to keep down, ride low ! Never saw a worse pair of make believe soldiers in my life! My God, what these men don't know about the rudiments of—"

"No one's about, Colonel," one of them tells me..

We're stopped now in a little ravine. And this troublemaker, Corey Everett's house is built on top of a hill, flanked by mountains of shale, rising sheer up, from different directions. No use to approach it by the main road.. But I can smell they've been drinking too much, must've filled their flasks last rest stop. I don't like it – a man needs a cold brain on the attack. What I'd really like, – take this Everett out of his place, hold a regular trial right here, hang him for cattle rustling, pretend it's all real legal. But we don't even know if he's home yet. And look at these damn Dallas wild men, bloodshot with corn rye, yelling and romping across Everett's grain field all spread out on either side of us down here. No good to order 'em off either, they can't hear

that far away ...And what in blazes are they doing now –
setting his grain afire? Yes, that's what it looks like, talk
about craziness! Now he'll sure be warned, if he's anywhere
in the neighborhood..

"Come on, Colonel!" cries Mr. Roy, JR., and looks like
he's drunk himself. So there they go, riding around wild,
burning his field, shooting off their guns. All but Roy's clerk,
Ridgley, and that silly Englishman who's got off his horse,
and I swear, is calmly drawing the whole thing. Just sitting
there drawing, and all those others shouting, restless with a
kind of drunken excitement. And here they come galloping
back now to where I sit, their hands stained with sheep
blood, all set for making a great rush towards the house.

Thank God, Roy Junior's still able to listen to reason.

"Keep 'em here while I reconnoiter," I say.

I ride up that trail, almost like a regular gorge it is,
with sheer rock rising from various sides, and I look up the
hill to Everett's house. No sign of life. Far as I can see his
barn's empty, no smoke in his chimney either, and all those
shades pulled down.

Well, we don't aim to hang around waiting for him to
come back. Just his good luck he isn't here, that's all. And if
he don't take the hint and ride straight out of Fargos county
after what we're going to do to his house...

"How about it, Colonel?" asks young Roy when I get back, the men grouped about him full of pumped up wildness from drinking, (the one named Blanding, –he with the hook hand– tossing empty bottles in the air and shooting 'em, bling, with only his left hand alone!)"We goin' to drag him out of there now?" asks Roy, rearing his black Pinto up.

Some picture we must have made! Ridgley behind me carrying the flag, me in front leading the charge, Roy on my left, and all of us shooting hell bent for that empty house. (I didn't tell 'em it was empty, what was the sense of spoiling their spirit? Anyways, an officer should always lead his troops.) So here we are, riding and shouting up that gorge and get to the place where it narrows between two big rocks, and all of a sudden heavy rifle fire starts coming from somewhere above the hill, more'n a few rifles too, and the next thing I know, my medals go *spang* as something hits me like a great hammer thrown by a bunch of men from atop a water tower or something...

"Take cover," I hear Roy yelling. "Take cover. Everybody take cover."

Then I don't hear anything anymore.

FIRST DAY

Such a sweet morning. Everything so bright and sunny, my fields down there beginning to look like they should have looked the last two years, high and sweet and wavy, and me with enough of my own feed for the first time in months. Well, it don't do a thing to me. Nothing ever turns out like you think it's going to. All that work we put in since coming here from Ohio, all those things plaguing us, drought and blight and floods and our poor sheep ailing and dying and those crazy cattlemen telling old wives' tales about what we're going to do to their graze, trying to shove us out and threatening us and calling us lying names, and even accusing us of rustling beef till sometimes more 'n words are called for – none of it was too much to bear.

But how about fever killing off a man's wife and boy in less than six day's time, the damn plains fever, giving no warning and laughing at prayers, and leaving two graves right where the grain's still green? All this acreage cleared, my ground beginning finally to look like something, my wool coming along fine this year, and now those two new mounds staring me in the face every time I take the plough down hill.

Well, maybe I was wrong. Perhaps I should've buried 'em in Buffalo, taken 'em away from here. Because it's too hard sometimes – working all day and coming home to this empty bed and them lying not fifty feet away in wooden boxes. No, I shouldn't've had that notion. Still, God in his good time, as they say. They can't call me a worshiper, but you take a man who's not a God-fearing man, he isn't apt to last long in a place like this. So what I aim to do is sweat myself to sleep each night, work all day, pray my memories'll ease. Because this can still be a proud enough place one day, and that's what I come out here for — to own my own land, make something out of it. If I could only just begin enjoying the act of working it again...

Hello. Wreck of a wagon coming up the hill, two people on it. Can't make 'em out clear at this distance. But what are they doing all this way off the road to Buffalo? Well company's one thing I don't hanker for right now, and looks like they got a boy with 'em too. Creaking right up to where I'm painting my well bucket and the man gets off. Short and spidery, sort of, and with a moustache. Sort of a dandified man, though he's dressed like anyone else.

"Howdy," he says. "This isn't Buffalo, is it?" laughing applause to his own joke., I just keep on workin..

"The name's Louis Finletter," he says, offering his hand. "My wife Amy, my boy Albie. Got lost riding up from the South, and then to top it off, King's foot starting ailing," nudging that starved horse of his.

I just keep on painting. Those other two haven't budged from the wagon.

"If we could maybe borrow a horse?" he says. "Or get a new shoe fitted for King? And as it's late, perhaps rest till sunup tomorrow. Because I don't hanker after night traveling again," he says, his fingers in his vest. "specially being as how we're strangers in these parts."

I don't see any occasion in speaking yet. But he goes on, telling that he's an itinerant tooth doctor, and if I need any work done...

"We'll pay cash money," a woman's voice says.

I look up. Thin, about thirty, and a boy of twelve or thirteen sitting next to her. But what's surprising is how they resemble each other, lean and clean looking, and both of them as different from him as black and white. "The barn'll do as well as the house for sleeping," she says in that flat voice.

So I finally let them come in. What's use's the house to me, anyway, and they said only for a night. But what angers me is to see how he's been beating that poor horse, and without even sense enough to take the shoe off, letting it run sore shod through the sage. So now he's close to

28

having a lame animal, and it's only through his dumbness or cruelty, I don't know which. And all through the afternoon what's he do but stand around, jawing a mile a minute about where he's been, and how he's going to set up in Buffalo, and how it's a shame I never been to New York City. On and on, enough to make you throw your food back up again. And all that time his wife and boy unpacking without him lifting one finger to help on account of his fingers, as he says, which he has got to take good care of, being as how they're his livelihood. Those other two don't make a sound, but you can see there's kinship between them, and like as if they were on one side and him on the other.

Well, none of my business. Come tomorrow, they'll be gone and good riddance! But late afternoon I walk away, while that woman's busy cleaning my pots. I tap him a little, but he don't wake up Finally I give him a little twist, meanin' only to move him off, but maybe my feeling gets the better of me, because he rolls too far over and goes plunk on the boards, waking up.

"What is it...?" he says blinking.

"Over there's where you sleep," I say, and notice all at once his boots made a tear through the coverlet Julia finished only last March. Oh I could've smashed him then for good!

"Sorry, brother," he says. "But there's no need for such – ah – agitated... ...."

"*Agitated*?" I begin. Only just then his boy, Albie, comes in, and walks straight over to me. Says he's been on the silo and seen a party of horsemen approaching from the South. Says he thought he could hear something, maybe firing. If we listen, maybe we'll be able to hear ourselves..

All at once we *do* hear something! Rifle shots, and mixed in with it, something like echoes of shouts, or it might have been just wind. I go out and start walking down hill, slow, telling them to keep inside the house. I know there's Indians loose in the territory, a fellow up North disappeared eight days ago, you never can tell. Or it might be outlaws from south of Claremont, coach was held up there not so long ago, too . Or even troublemakers from the cattle farms tryin' to worry me again, they done it before. In this county anything's liable to happen.

But before I can get to the bottom of the hill and see, right in front of me smoke begins to rise, and then more smoke. Why goddam them, they're firing my land! All that rifle fire and so much shouting, I can't make it out. But what I know is I better keep close to the cliff wall, else they'll see me, and whoever it is don't mean me any good for sure! Though if it's Indians liquored up, firing my fields may be

30

enough to discourage 'em for a spell. Sometimes they do just that, – steal a few sheep, and ride on before you can get a fair shot at 'em. But by the noise, there's too many this time, so I run back up the hill and start trying to arrange some kind of camouflage. Luckily, my place's way up high where there's a kind of cave in the granite behind it, and I put the horses in there and my creaky wagon too, and hope whoever it is'll think I'm off somewhere.

Inside the house, that woman's got a nice fire beginning but I pour a bucket of water on it and throw a rug after. Steam sloshes all around.

"Here, what're you doing?" she says, and her husband in shirt sleeves comes up, and that boy of theirs stands next to me. He's been helping me all the while, driving the stock behind the house and pushing with the wagon.

"If it's Indians, a cold chimney might set 'em off," I say. "And us here on the top of this hill might even discourage 'em from climbing up."

"Indians!" yells her husband, whining like a sick goat "Indians!"

All of us rushing around inside there, drawin' down shades, filling clips, and he just keeps sort of running around, saying that word to himself over and over: ?Indians, Indians." Till finally I put a rifle in his hand.

31

"Here now," he said "I don't never fired one of these..."

Luckily that old shotgun and two extra hunting rifles we had were in place where I stored 'em away. So in a few minutes time, quicker'n you could imagine, here we are, the four of us kneeling in the dark, that twelve year old too, with guns in our hands, and the front windows shaded by all but an inch at the bottom for viewing.

"But what are we going to do?" he's still groaning. "If it's Indians, and I aint never fired one of these..."

"Just pull the trigger is all."

"Oh, oh, oh." he says, sighing like a woman. You never seen such a weak gizzard in all your life.

But those other two are silent. And now we can't hear too much down in the hollow either. But waiting, we see one figure come riding up the gorge, dim, he keeps back under the bank. His face's too far away to be seen. But it's no Indian, that's sure, and he's got some kind of uniform on, I can't make it out...

Then he goes away. We kneel waiting. A crazy situation in a way, –these three Finletters and myself holding gun point to marauders, or *whatever* they are,. strangers at that. And meanwhile that whining, ninny of a man who might have belonged to another family much as he resembled those other two – him groaning over and over.

"How long're we going to have to wait? Oh I knew I shouldn't have turned in this direction!. How long before we'll find out whether-"

But he was answered soon enough, and not by me! Because in a few minutes here come's a wild bunch of men charging up the hill like some kind of military posse with a flag too, and at the head a big man in a confederate uniform, and riding a white horse.

"Not yet." I whisper around in that dark. "Wait till they get to the narrow part where those black boulders come together. Because it narrows so only one or two can get through at a time. So wait a minute..., wait till they start tryin to crowd through that gorge and —   "Alright, now! Fire!" I tell them.

PERCY KETTERING

I wish I knew what was happening up on that hill. Yes, I can hear rifle fire, but it seems to be slackening now. Have they captured the blighter? Bit of bad luck, to have to stay

33

here alone like this, but the way I ride that bloody animal of mine, what else could I do?

Yet I must say, the whole thing's confusing. I mean, why do they have to go burning up the fellow's grain? Even if he is what they call a rustler and so on, this grain could have still been used, couldn't it? And the way these men disport themselves, drinking, shouting, arguing, why I almost believe they care as much for their flasks as for punishing vandals. Just simple American justice to rustlers, Roy said. Well, perhaps I'm just not used to this American violence, because, my word, the way these gentlemen work themselves up,! And then...

Hello, here they come riding back down the hill again. And what's that they're carrying – *bodies?* Yes, the Colonel must be shot! I can see the sun glinting off his gold buttons. But where's Roy? Didn't they even get to the house? I say, Roy, Roy!

No one seems to be answering at all. Oh now there he is, poor chap, draped over that black horse. A nasty wound too, right in the center of his chest. But these others don't seem to care, no one's doing anything for him at all! And there's the poor Colonel, un-conscious by the looks of it, they've lowering him to the ground, the sun shining off his two fancy revolvers. And here's Mr. Ridgley standing on the supply wagon all of a sudden, making a kind of speech.

"The first thing we have to do," he says, "is give Colonel Samson and this other man a decent burial. Then I want camp struck for the night and guards posted, and in the morning we'll make another attack from..."

"Wait a minute," interrupts the man they call Hook. "Who's giving the orders...?"

"Mr. Roy, Sr. designated me third in command, Sir. And since unfortunately the Colonel and young Mr. Roy..."

"You,?" cries Blanding. "In *command*?"
Evidently this seems to be the signal for rather widespread amusement, because everyone but Mr. Ridgley laughs. And then Mr. Hook turns rather impolitely, ignoring Mr. Ridgley.

"Maybe we ought to strike camp at that," he says. "Night's coming on, we don't know these parts. Those men up there in the house aint going to pull anything till sunup anyway, and by then we can be far away from..."

"Mr. Blanding," says Ridgley. "I would like to remind you, everyone present has signed an agreement."

"Mighty beautiful guns," says Blanding, looking to where poor Colonel Samson lies, his two holsters turned outwards in kind of a harness shape.

"I warn you Sir!," cries Ridgley. "Mr. Roy designated me third in command. All this property is under my jurisdiction. And—"

"Get me those guns, will you Sal?" says Mr. Hook to one of the other men.

"I'm warning you, again, Sir, whoever touches Colonel Samson's things..."

It all happens so quickly I can hardly believe it! The man called Sal reaching forward, Mr. Ridgley with his hand out, his own pistol firing before anyone can move! And all of us staring at the ground where the Sal gentleman is now sprawled upon a reddening stain.

Mr. Hook bends once and straightens up. "Dead!" he says.

"I warned you, I told you Mr. Roy designated me third in command..."

"You,! cries Mr. Hook. "*You?*"

His left hand makes one movement, so fast I can't follow it. But Mr. Ridgley's faster! When he fires a second time, he shoots that pistol right out of Mr. Hook's hand!..

"As I said, Sir, third in command."

We all stand there, gaping. Darkness starting to cover these hills all around now. And I don't know whether it's from cold or fright that my silly legs begin to tremble.

36

Because here we are, all these Texans with hands on their guns. And that little man standing there, apt to shoot as well as speak. And here's poor Roy,– lying nearby on a saddle blanket, his voice moaning away....

"Mr. Blanding," says Ridgley, still with both guns free. "You are hereby appointed my deputy. I want these bodies buried and camp struck, also guards posted. And in thirty minutes, come to my tent for instructions."

With that, he turns his back and walks off. Ten men could've shot at him before he moved ten feet, he would've been dead a hundred times over, but his guns are still free, and no one makes a single move.

Everyone just looks after him, staring.

HOOK

Crazy, that's all! Plain loco out of his head!... To shoot Sal through the heart like *that*, only because of two lousy guns.? And my fingers still trembling for what happened after. Well, the only thing is to *humor* him,–it's only for one night... Because in the morning I don't intend to stay around for long, where's the sense? We got half the money and a horse, and what do I care about risking my neck on the hill again tomorrow...

When I report to him though, I'm careful to put on a good show, because the little high and mighty is sitting there in his tent with the Colonel's two guns on either side and the Colonel's cap on his head.

"Guards posted," I tell him, and see him jump up, excited.

"Mr. Blanding" he says, and he's taken one of those guns off the table, so I'm careful to seem real respectful. "I'm under no delusions as to your loyalties," he says. "but I would like to point out to you certain things. We were sent on this little expedition to apprehend five men, and we seem to have run into more than five right here at Everett's place. Which means that if we don't clean out the house up there, they'll be able to give an alarm throughout the whole county and not only will Mr. Roy's money and purpose be thwarted, but all these damn homesteaders will have gained a reason to make heroes out of themselves. Another thing, as you know,--we are a day's ride at the least from Claremont., And I doubt whether we could reach there without interception because any division of this party would also increase the danger that the men on the hill'd be able to make a counterattack. Also, I don't intend to betray Mr.

38

Roy's own purposes. I intend to carry out this undertaking as originally charged ."

I don't bat one eye. "Yes sir," I say, everything but a salute in my eyes.

"But since I do not expect everyone to appreciate my purposes, Mr. Blanding, no more I do yourself," he goes on, "I am prepared to make certain gestures. Of which *this*," he says, throwing a little bag on the table, "is the first."

I pick it up. Gold. Heavier than a handful. And for *me*, he says, if I'll spread the word about how all those men attacking the hill tomorrow'll receive twice their original pay, plus a fair share of all sums remanded both by those two who left us yesterday, and by poor Sal and Bye who got shot in the charge today. "Plus the praise and honor of all true cattlemen in Fargos county," he says, imitating the dead Colonel.

Suddenly I begin to see a glimmering. Fifteen men times two a hundred apiece, and what if there's only four or five left to divide it? But I have to be careful. Because right now the thing to do is play make-believe, go along with Ridgley's Military masquerade, acting as if he were General Grant. Especially while he's got those pistols in his hands.

But then as we're sitting there in his tent we hear a commotion outside, rifle shots, and in a few seconds Big

Joe Ramos comes crashing in, dragging a little skinny poor excuse of a man by the elbow. Black mustache, white face, mouth babbling and babbling.

"Found him trying to sneak around by the fire," Jose says. "Trying to steal one of our horses."

"Oh no, I assure you, Sir," the runt babbles.

"I was only trying to tell someone,– aint me's about to steal any horses! Oh no Sir, I wouldn't do *that*," he says. "Finletters the name," he rushes on, "Louis Finletter. If there's anyone here has a toothache..."

Ridgley gets up. I swear, the man begins to quiver as if he was about to have something good to eat.

"Mr. Blanding, " he says. "Tie the prisoner to a chair."

"*Prisoner? Me?* Oh no Sir," this runt yells. "I don't know who you gentlemen are, but if you could do me the kindness of listening to my story ...–..."

"How many in the house up there?" asks Ridgley in a soft voice.

Candles on the table, Ramos and me to one side, that runt sweating and squirming, his back tied to a folding chair. And all the while Ridgley conducting what he calls his "interrogation."

"We was just passing through this territory, Sir,... that is... my wife and boy. and myself, And happened to lose our way , somehow, when--."

"Mr. Blanding!," cries Ridgley, in a strange voice. "I think you ought to "encourage" the prisoner a little.."

"No, no, no!" cries the poor runt. "As I said, I was only trying to get away, --it's only the three of us, my wife and my son, and me.. And whatever else happens to be going on around here, ... we e don't know nothing about that, sir, we was only looking for a place to rest so that we could--.."

"Mr. Blanding!" cries Ridgely, giving me my cue.

I have to do it I. He's watching me, and Ramos too, and besides, this runts whining somehow starts to get on my nerves. But it's more the sight of the hook than anything else, because I don't really cut him very bad. Ridgley meanwhile's rocking back and forth, Ramos gravely shaking his head, and finally the runt begins to break down

"Please, please, please, "he says," God's truth, we only happen to be passing through, as I said. And our horse is lame. So if you could let us purchase one of yours, we'll be only too happy to - -"

"How many men are up there in that house --right now -- ten, twelve...?"

41

"AS I said, sir, I don't really know how to.. Ow! Please, make him stop doing that, sir ! Tell him to quit jabbing me with whatever it is he's using.. ——"

"Mr. Blanding," says Ridgley. "Untie the prisoner." The rope's pretty wet from all the sweat he's been staining his clothes with, every time Ridgley signals me to use the Hook again. But now he starts running madly towards the tent entrance

"Free?" says Ramos objecting. "Free...!"

You never saw such shooting in your life!. Right from the open tent by the light of that half moon, crazy Ridgley takes aim and brings that running figure down with one clean shot through the chest! Then he sits down right away, and begins writing something in a little black book.

"Penalty of death for spying," he says. "Sentence carried out, 12:41 A.M."

COREY EVERETT

In the darkness I can't make out the others too well. But Albie, the boy's sound asleep beside me. Then I hear a sound. I draw the bolt back.

42

"Don't shoot," Finletter whispers. "I...I was only going to go for help."

In a second my eyes get focused again. Sure enough, he's there, by the door, his hand on the knob, and I can see his eyes green with fear. Something else in them too, – a crazy look,I don't have a word to describe it...

"You ain't going to get very far," I tell him. "Not at night, not knowing anything about the terrain and without a horse..."

"I'll take one of theirs," he says. "Because you said they're maybe going to make another attack when it's light and then perhaps it'll be too late..."

All set to make a break for it by himself! How do you like that ?!. And without even asking the way, without even knowing the trails hereabouts !, So I see what he wants: to save *himself. period*!. And no thought about those other two, his *own* flesh and blood! Well, it's not my business to teach anybody else what his duty's *supposed* to be!... But makes you sick in the stomach just the same.

After he slips off, I don't hear anything for a while. 12:30. 1 o'clock. Albie, the boy's sleeping like a baby. I can't see whether his Ma is sleeping or not. Her rifle's still pointed under the shade. The moon makes a reflection off it.

2 o'clock. 3 o'clock. Can't doze any more. Is it really marauders? No, they're too well organized for that. And what kind of a flag were they carrying? Well if it's cattle stealers? No, Sheep *raisers*, more likely!. But where'd all those riders come from?

Well, I told them at Buffalo last month we ought to have some kind of warning system setup. Not only against occasional Indians, because everyone knows how some ranchers've been trying to run the rest of us out of this county, jealous of the acreage we're taking, even though it's legal by law. Thousands of head of their own, and they're still jealous of our small stake!. Well, we got a right to stay on our own land!....

Look at that boy Albie,—sleepin' away so good. Only a few years older than my Larry was. And he's a good boy too, with more spunk than his old man, by far... What time is it now?...Four o'clock? Well, must be quite a party down there by the light from all of all those fires. But that gives me an idea: how about all those firecrackers I brought back from Buffalo? No use to me lying in a cellar, and Larry ain't never goin' to see them anyway.

I'd need a long fuse line. I could slip out in the dark, maybe hug the cliff face, scatter a few of those big crackers

44

around. No but then how would I set 'em off? .... And might get caught at that.

Suddenly I get a better idea. I walk over to where the woman is.

But right away her bolt slips back. She hasn't been sleeping at all.

"Three feet's easy range," she says, her voice absolutely flat. It riles me to have that barrel pointed in my direction, and us in trouble enough. But damn her!. She must've heard him go off , too. And not sayin' one word to stop him !.... Even if he was trying to save his *own* skin, there's the boy to think about, isn't there? So what they must've felt for each other is worse than words can tell. I feel foolish, the pity I've wasted.

"All I want's something to stretch between two sticks," I say, "because I aim to try making a sling, Ma'am. If we can make them think there's more men outside..."

"Something to stretch between two sticks?"

"Like in ladies' garters, Ma am," I tell her.

She turns her back. It's still plenty dark, but not too dark so I can't see what she's doing. And when she turns back, they are in her hand.

"If you're looking for your husband..."

"I seen him go," she says. And still not a flicker of feeling in the woman...well, it ain't my affair. But I never saw such a cold stone of a female in my life. And while we're sitting there, me working on that sling, the light beginning to spread on the mountain and cliffs around, we hear a single horse plodding up through that gorge.

Both of us look through the window the same instant as up between the narrow pass comes one animal, and on it her husband, slumped over in what we know ain't no temporary pose. Both his hands are tied behind him, his face fallen to one side like a butchered calf. But when he gets closer we can see he's got a big sheet of printed foolscap pinned to his shirt, and that horse trots right near the window, pawing round the steps outside, so we can read it plain.

"Death To Rustlers" it says.

MRS. AMY FINLETTER

All the scrapes he got us into, and all the suffering, stretchin' the truth of a deck of cards till more'n one Sheriff give us twenty-four hours to move, and now look at him, deader'n a door knob! .. Well, whoever done it must've had his reasons although I don't figure on us getting entangled in whatever blood feuds may be ragin in these parts, though right now getting safely out of here has to be our number one priority. And as for the tight-lipped host who owns the place, —fussing as I say with some decrepit firecrackers he found in the cellar, and keeping to his surly and secretive self,— I'd wager he's been through some kind of hurtful personal experience he somehow still don't want to talk about, or aint yet found ways to come to terms with. Which could have something to do with why some of his neighbors —if they *are* his neighbors –keep trying to make life miserable for him, in whatever ways neighbors sometimes think up, once they've made up their minds to get rid of somebody the whole community is down on, for one reason or another.

. Whatever the reasons , I don't figure on us staying around here and finding ourselves accidentally being in the line of fire, whether intended or not

So the first thing I do is tear my petticoat and make a white cloth you can see from fifty yards away at least, and wake up my sleeping boy.

"Come on, Albie," I tell him. "You and I are going to take a walk down the hill pretty soon now..."

"Where's Pa?" he asks

47

I tell him what happened straight out. "Shot for a cattle thief," I say.

"Cattle thief?"

"Just stay close by " I say, "because I don't want you hanging too close to the character who owns this place, and, in some ways, may be responsible for what happened to your Pa. for all we know ......"

The three of us look at each other. But then Mr Everett goes back to whatever it is he's doing though Albie keeps following him around.. asking embarrassing questions like: "is she saying the truth, Mister?"

That boy! I would've slapped him if he were closer! But Everett simply ignores the both of us as usual and keeps on layin all those rusty-looking firecrackers he's been playing with in neat rows.

"You Albie," I say. " Try and open the door, now, for me, Okay?."

Outside the window the wind starts kickin' up, the yard is spurting with little gusts of dust. It had started out bright and sunny, but now it seems to be clouding up everywhere. Windows rattling, the roof shaking, and that stubborn boy of mine pestering Everett, or whatever he calls himself, despite what I told him. .

: "What are you doing with those old fire crackers, Mister? Are you going to shoot em off ?"

I know I have to act somehow.. But when I kick open the front door myself... wind and dust come flying into the room, I didn't realize how much the wind had begn to blow, so my rifle almost gets blown out of my hands. Part of my white petticoat goes sailing off into the yard.

"Albie, y'hear me?"

"What're you going to do with those firecrackers, Mister?"

I point the gun at them. Now outside the wind begins making such a sudden racket, you have to shout to be heard...

"Albie!"

"Put that gun away, don't point it at us", Everett tells me

"You let my boy alone..."

"I'm not saying anything to him ," he says. "But please, Maam, quit pointin' that gun in our direction..."

"You let him come along with me..."

"I ain't tellin' him what to do, ma-am."

"Ma," Albie says. He gets in front of the gun muzzle." It's Okay, Ma..

I really didn't mean for the dam thing to go off ! But what with that wind blowing outside and us shouting at one another, and that man's face so scornful looking, I really can't say how it happened.. The room suddenly thundered! Then a hand comes smashing across my arm, and I fall down, the same time as Albie starts in shouting, "Ma, Ma, Ma..."

But it was the *other* one, Everett himself, had been shot, and knocked me down too. And now he goes and takes the other half of my petticoat lying on the floor, wrapping a bandage about his hurt shoulder, never saying a word all the time. And in a few minutes here he is, talking' to Albie again, and my own boy helping me to my feet.

"I need you to help me with something,"he says to Albie

"What'd you hit her for, she didn't know what she was doing?"

"Why I had to do it, boy!. She might've killed either one of us..."

"I didn't like for you to do that."

"You ready to help me, boy?"

And now the wind's getting louder.. And there's another sound,— yelling and firing it sounds like , echoing from way down the hill. And before I know how it happens,

50

here I am by the same window, and him with his bandaged arm giving Albie my garters tied to sticks, and taking a gun himself.

"Don't light 'em and sling 'em off until I say so," he tells Albie. " We got to make them think there's a crowd up here."

"Remember, it's has to be way up in the air, and to the right.! That's it. you got the idea!... Now just hold on a sec, -hold on, hold on---"

"Okay, *Now*!" he says.We watch. Crack! There's a little burst to the right of that path off down the hill. And then another in the air! And another!

"Take your time, boy," Everett says. "That's it. You're doing fine!"

PERCY KETTERING

"Poppies, poppies... I like poppies best. If you have to plant flowers at all, Ma..."

"Roy! Listen to me..."

"Not ride Tiger? Me not ride that stupid horse? Why since when do you think I can't..."

"It's Kettering," I tell him. " Listen to me, Roy.. Roy..."

51

No use. He doesn't hear. Just keeps tossing on that cot, mumbling in delirium. And this bloody tent shivering like a banshee in the wind. But I say, all this is rather different from what I expected. That Ridgley chap is , plainly, not quite all "*there*" ! ….. Walking around like some clown in a bloody circus, burlesquing a General!, Making the men line up in military squads for what he calls his "inspection." And those two men he appointed under him, Hook and that Ramos chap, strutting after him like a couple of bloody Subalterns. And now this wild storm.

But meanwhile, here's poor Roy burning up. " Send someone for help at least, "I tell Ridgley. But the blighter doesn't seem to hear!. "That poor chap needs doctoring ! He's losing blood every single sec—"

"*Casualties*?" Ridgley shouts. "Do you think I'm not suffering with the thought of my own men's casualties !

"But why not try to get help for ….?"

"*I'm* the one knows this terrain," he shouts. "And *I'm* in charge here!. Do you think I dare trust anyone else? Most'd probably run off and either get themselves lost or injure their horse somehow….And maybe even head straight for the authorities…..!

"The *authorities*? I don't understand… Why should you care if …"

52

"Never mind, no more questions!" the blighter hollers. "I have to plan strategy... There's probably more than ten men up there..... And if they knew how *few* of us were down here.."

"But Sir...?

"*Adjutant!* he yells, though all of these chaps were only civilians to start with , far as I know. But one of them, a huge Mexican chap, comes and escorts me out of the tent, and I have to go back and sit with Roy.

Lord, this wind is really frightful. And poor Roy still babbling all kinds of nonsense. But how can I help him, what to do?

Then all at once he sits straight up on the bed, feverish, and begins yelling at me.

"Kettering! Is that you, Kettering? I want you to do something, — you hear? Tell the old man he was right! I I was wrong in not supporting him 100 percent I. Even if we have to accuse every damn homesteader of rustling, I don't care I Let's hang em all from their cow barns, run 'em out, all of them I Because we gave them warning, we told them to get out, didn't we? A man has a right to own what he first fought over!. So where are you Kettering, I can't see you!.., Kettering, Kettering..."

Wild and screaming he is, and trying to get up off that cot, and I have to really fight the poor chap to hold him down. Then all at once he goes limp, his breathing rattles. But I can't say I'm much stronger myself. The truth is he just admitted it, he said it straight out!....Nothing but a gang of rogues,& mercenaries is what they all are, —the whole lot of them ! So that's what explains the whole bloody ...

But I don't have time to think Because just the0 the wind gives a shriek and something crashes down somewhere and I rush outside.

Ood. what a bloody whirling filthy cloud of dust, stones and dirt!. Two of the tents are already down., All of a sudden I think: horses, horses!. If Ridgley was planning to have them charge the hill on *foot* later on, and without horses —

I rush up past the half-torn down tents, the wind and sand tearing at my face and eyes, but my word, what kind of a storm do they call this, where does that bloody *hail* come from? When I come near Ridgley's tent where the horses are tethered, I find groups of men running around, trying to calm whatever excited animals haven't tried to stampede already . And yelling among themselves...

"I told you we should've tethered them lower down ,I knew this spot was too high up...,"

",Never mind, we got to secure as many as we can.!."

"Of all the bloody crazy schemes !, , Must've been half a dozen of Everett's pals waiting for us up there, maybe even outside the house , making us dead giveaways soon's they spotted us!"

And Ridgley meanwhile, sitting on his bloody gelding, watching everything through his bloody field glasses!

"By God, *where is* that murderous little bastard ! I'd like to get my hands on his—"

"No, no forget that!,— We have to save *that* for later !...Right now, keep reaching for any reins you're lucky enough to grab hold of...!"

None of us can't see hardly ten feet ahead of ourselves ! But groping my way down, luckily, I find our tent's still intact. Still, half-crazed with fear and anger, though, I can't help shouting at Roy as if he were actually able to hear what I'm saying ... "More than half the horses gone! " I shout! "Canteens gone with them.!And two more men with serious wounds, left up on the hill!..., So what am I supposed to think of the "honorable" Squire now , hey ? I mean, even a bloody thick-headed Englishman like me can finally recognize it when he's finds he's been marooned amongst a pack of plain plunderers, – - getting ready to murder innocent men!—"

Roy doesn't hear what I'm telling him of course—doesn't even move. Suddenly I lean over the cot.

Blank, rigid, frozen his eyes are, cold as stones! No heart beat at all. The boy is dead.

"Leave that window open."

"But the dust, it'll choke us in here."

"You leave that window be," Mr. Everett says.

He's stood up and him and Ma are still glaring at each other across the room. So then I have to sneeze, because there's so much dust coming in from outside now and he wouldn't let Ma close the windows for fear we couldn't fire quick enough if we had to.. I bet it's Indians he's worrying about.. — I bet he's seen plenty of fights with Indians before, too, only Ma don't know anything about it, how could she, we never seen Indians back home, 'cept in the funny papers. And then he said he has something important he wants me to do and is going to tell me what it is..

Only when I start sneezing again, like as if I'm choking or something, , he closes one window halfway..

"You're letting my son near choke to death!," Ma shouts.

"Better than letting him be shot by outlaws, Ma am."

"*Outlaws*? Please, let's not start talking about *"outlaws..!"* she cries.

But Mr Everett doesn't answer.. Just sits there pounding away at what looks like a sort of piece of old stove pipe.

"Bringing you to legal account—though I don't know what for I —is what they do to types like yourself I" Ma tells him, though we all have to keep yelling to hear one another above the noise of the dust and wind and hail..

"Why not try to get some sleep, Maam?"

"Sleep? And you and that boy whispering together,I *still* don't know what about I I..Well, you won't be talkin very long. As soon as that storm clears, we're going to walk down that hill."

"Suit yourself Ma am."

After a while I try talking to her.

"Ma... Please"

"Not right now, Please, Albie, I'm trying to think..

"But Ma..."

"In a minute, Albie, I got to try to get something straight in my head.."

We never seen anything like this storm. Stones and everything swirling all around, I think it's better'n a tornado. But I'm hungry, haven't had hardly anything to eat all day... Meanwhile, Ma and him are just sittin' there, she with her gun in one hand, and him pounding that piece of stove pipe. What's he doing that for? And that bandage on his arm getting redder'n redder.

"I'm hungry, ma."

"You'll just have to wait a little bit, Albie. Till we get out of this..."

"But Ma.."

"There's a little bread left," Mr. Everett says. "Nothing much else right now. Because today is when I was planning to go into Buffalo for supplies"

But when I start in chewing fast, he stops me.

"Not so fast, boy. You don't want to make yourself too thirsty. Because we're going to be in trouble after this storm let's up, our water's real low. And my Well's way on the other side of the hill ; that's why, we can't risk getting any till night fall."

"Nightfall?" shouts Ma. "We're not going to be spending another night in this place.."

"Suit yourself Ma am."

"It's okay, Ma," Albie says..."

"Risk getting killed for no reason?" she turns on me. "We *still* don't know what they got against our sour-faced host here! And didn't they just kill your own Pa for reasons we don't know zero about?"

"You said we'd find out later, Ma, when—"

"Whoever he was, remember — and forgetting his failures as a family man—he never done something they could actually arrest him for !.So when this storm clears-"

"I aint t going down there with you, Ma."

"See what you're doing!," she shouts at Everett.. "A child's blood on your hands, — is that what you want-? Turning my own son against me!..."

"Please, You're scaring the boy, Ma am."

"Hey, storm's stopping," I tell them. They look at me. Outside, the wind is weaker, the sun's coming through.

But God, am I hungry.

SECOND DAY

When Ridgley calls for me to come to his tent, and all
that dust and wind still howling outside, I loose my pistol in
it's holster. Because a portion of our drinking water's gone,
and there's only so many horses left , the rest must've
stampeded in the storm. Meanwhile, he's still playing Mr
high and mighty like some sort of stage Emperor or
something. I've a notion to tell him how truly crazy he is
right to his face, but with a trigger happy type like he is,
you've got to be careful.. One or two bad-sounding words
striking him the wrong way, and whammo ! You're apt to
find yourself flat on your face, a bullet in your arm or elbow
and him explaining just which "military tradition" you've
violated, and what kind of "apology" he's waiting to hear.

"Mr. Blanding," he says, both of his guns still
within reach, "Have the men fall out. Young Mr. Roy's dead.
A hero's death too, in battle it was, and his father'd be
proud. So we have to stand to, putting him below ground."

I don't make a move. Nor a sound either. His eyes
look grey from no sleep in almost forty-eight hours.

"I said have the men fall out, Mr. Blanding."

"They ain't going to."

"I'm not *asking* whether they're going to. You tell them that's an *order!*."

"I reckon that's going to make less of a point than a pint of water would right now," I say. "They're not fixing to take orders from you any more."

He looks straight at me. Sure, he could shoot, but then again, he mightn't be so lucky this time. Anyways, he ain't fixing to do it. His eyes are shrewd as gophers'.

"Are you trying to admit I've made a mistake in choosing deputies, Mr. Blanding? Or can't you control them, even you if you wanted?"

"They ain't fixing to get themselves killed anymore for no crowd of brand stealers!... And I ain't going to do any persuading..."

Him on one side of the table, and me on the other. He looking at me, studying-like. I with my left hand fingers an inch from the holster.

"The point is," he says. "We're going to have to get rid of that crowd on the hill now or our own lives are apt to be remarkably short. Because this hill territory is right now sand blown, Mr. Blanding, and the only one who could take us to where we might ride to Claremont is myself. In addition to which, if we leave, they'll see what our *real* situation is. But in any case I intend to remain faithful to the purposes of the

Squire. Everyone here was hired to implement those purposes."

"Not to get killed because someone's got a yearn to play General Whosis," I finally say. "And with our water gone and most of the horses too..."

"Mr. Blanding," Ridgley says, casual, as if he's announcing the time of day. "You better not move. Because I just noticed there's a rattler on the floorboard about three inches behind your left foot Remain perfectly still, don't budge. If we both stay still, he may not bother you."

The tent suddenly gets hot, my clothes feel greasy. I can't tell whether he's trying to trip me or not. If he is, and I turn around, he'll shoot sure., But if I pull my own colt and he ain't lying, my life ain't worth a nickel from snake bite. So standing there and shivering I am, and the little General talking to me in a whisper, and all the while that howling still going on outside.

"I want you to tell the men to fall out," he says.

"And you might also tell them that their best chance for water is Everett's Well, and his horses, too. Because all of them in the house up there didn't come on foot, they must have their animals quartered behind the rise where we can't see from down here. Also, we should start digging for water ourselves today, as soon as this wind stops, and it may be there's veins in shallow ground around here

Now all I'm going to ask is whether or not you'll agree to use your—uh—powers of *persuasion* in these matters or not. Because I'm quite willing either to shoot straight at the snake's head or miss by only a few inches.

In which case," he says, "we both know what'll probably happen."

Nothing comes out of me. I keep telling myself he's bluffing, and quit saying a word. But my damn foot's trembling so, I'm afraid it's going to rattle the board, and I can already feel the fangs in my ankle. I was bitten by a rattler once, I almost didn't make it. Another thing, though I hate his guts, what he says makes more sense than stealing a horse and running off in this damn wilderness alone !. Besides, how'd I know he ain't rigged some kind of signal to let the Squire know? So I shake my head up and down twice, and keep my eyes pinpointed. In all that howling wind outside I can't hear any rattling at all.

A split second is all it takes !. One shot, and then boom! I turn. Stretched, writhing and bloody and still squirming, with its awful head blown to a thousand pieces and splattered to hell and gone, is the ugliest biggest bastard of a rattler you ever saw!

I don't say a thing, go right out into the dust and wind, heave my guts all over the ground,. When I look back inside, he's reloading.

Oh if only I could get rid of this damn bullet! My shoulder's beginning to throb again. If I could only get it out!. But all we got's that little amount of water left. And she's sitting there, that gun still pointed this way, no telling what she'd do if I was to kind of doze a little. Well, I don't give a damn, let her go and get shot, what's that to me? A man is always infringed upon !. There I was, minding my business, and all this come to me, I didn't do a thing to bring it on. Right now, my head don't feel none too great. I swear, if the boy and her don't stop arguing, I may have to smack both their heads together.

"I told you we're going," she says to Albie. "Let's not argue about it."

"No, Ma, I'm not going.."

"What's come over you, Albie ? You want to see us killed?"

"I don't care what you say, Mr. Everett's no cattle rustler for sure...."

"They shot your Pa, didn't they, thinking it was *him* ? Or is my word of no account to you these days .....?"

"I'm just saying, Everett's no Rustler, that's all."

"Look –I'm not going to argue with you about it, Albie. I'm _telling_ youl. Please help me open the front door so we can—"

"You can't make me, Ma..."

"Can't make you,– CAN'T MAKE YOU! What's got into you, Albie Finletter...? Talking to your own Ma that way!

Just then, I decide it's time for me to quit playing around with my stove pipe and come over to where they're both of them standing, the two of them. I know my face looks bad..I've been rubbing that improvised bandage on my shoulder –as if I were trying to make the pain go way. But my voice is lower than most people're used to, I think, – as if it were hurting me to talk., That's why that boy can hardly understand what I'm tryin to say,–"

"You got a strong stomach, boy?"

"I swear I'll shoot this rifle off," his Ma starts in... But that plucky boy manages to get between the two of us. She's bristling with rage by now, of course but it don't do any good. Meanwhile, I feel my strength ebbing away,it goes and it comes. If only I could catch a spell of sleep.

"I need you to do something special for me, Albie, " I say.

"Albie," his Ma shouts. "WE're going down that hill to find out who's shooting up at this house , whether night or day, it don't even seem to matter which .. But if you won't come with me..."

"Take this knife I'm holding," I'm meanwhile explaining to Albie." See where that blood's soaking through my shoulder ? Well, I can't even reach over and deal with those bandages with only one hand....."

"Albie...I"his Ma calls again

When she calls his name this time,I can't help it, I pick up a piece of fire-wood and hurl it at her to make her shut up ! Which makes that rifle she's carrying go off a *second* time, *-* -BANG ! Which makes the weapon start jerking and sliding across the floor.. Both her and the boy are scrambling for it now—But Albie's quicker., He throws it over to me and I hand it back to her. . Then she flings herself on the floor, sitting against that logged wall, sobbing to herself.[1]

"Oh Albie, Albie!... you don't know what you're doing... putting yourself at risk for a possible criminal like him?."

"You fixin' to do what I'm asking, boy?"

Albie looks at me. His lips are pale, he's sweating. But his eyes don't waver.. Then suddenly, his Ma decides to start reading from the bible my wife Julia bought last year from a

---

store in Buffalo. On her knees,I swear, over in a corner, mumbling like it was the end of the world or something. Meanwhile, I'm trying to teach Albie what he needs to learn...

"See where it's bleeding there, boy?. Course, we have to get those bandages off quick as possible..."

He's staring at me, wetting his lips while he listens.. Then he moves. Puts his hand out. And slowly unwraps a piece of that blood-soaked petticoat. What he sees ain't too tolerable to him, it seems, from the way his face grimaces for a second or two

"*Blessed are thy faithful true servants*," his Ma's now reading aloud from the Holy Book over in a corner. "*Blessed are they that serve Thee....Blessed be those who succor Thy children...etc..*"

", Aint no disgrace if you can't do it, boy" I tell him. ". But I can hardly manage, to deal with the wound with only one of my hands available.. So if you can just make the first cut. It's the bullet that's wedged in, that's draining my strength away.. Better bring in a bucket of water, too, one of those we were saving for drinking. Right now, don't look like drinking is what we need to give most priority to......."

"Albie, dear, " murmurs his Mama in a subdued tone.. Then she turns her attention to prayer once more.

70

"Oh Lord, make Thy innocent servants heart to melt" she murmurs. ".

"You think you can do it, boy?" I finally ask...

He still don't move, just stands there looking at me, with the pain coming and going and his Ma murmuring from Julia's bible. Sun so bright now and no one coming up through the gorge yet...But how long our luck will hold up is anyone's guess...

"You sure you can stand it, Mr. Everett?" Albie asks me

"Don't worry," I tell him." Just work the flesh little by little. I can feel it up near that shoulder bone. But you better heat up some water first, as we ought to try to make everything as sanitary as we can.."

He does it all by himself. Takes the pot., Makes the fire. Heats that water up. All the while his Mama's sort of talking to herself and looking at both of us.

"Ah Albie, Albie," she says. "It's all my fault, I brung you to this. It was me wanted to come out here. After all the trouble your Pa got us into back in Illinois, it was myself wanted us to make a fresh start. But you're acting like a stranger this minute., I don't know even who I'm really talking to..."

71

"Take the knife, boy," I tell him. "And that fry pan too, case of spillover. I'll hold on with the other hand."

He takes the hot water and puts it on the floor. Then swathes that blade around. Then puts the point to skin. I like to faint at first. Have to keep swearing inside and cussing like anything. Oh it's terrible! Goddam those sons-of-bitches besieging us from the valley. He sees me sweating buckets, too, and stops.

"What's the matter boy?"

"You sure you're alright, sir . I mean you don't look too good..."

"A little weakness come up in me...is all," I tell him." But don't stop. Keep on going..

"Albie", his Ma pleads. "You oughtn't to be fiddling around with wounds and such at your age. And God forbid, if something unforeseen should happen—"

At this, Albie suddenly stops. Gives me an inquiring look—as if to say, is everything okay ?

"Hey, you can't quit right in the middle," I tell him. "You're doing fine. Just a little more to the right, and we're home free." Albie takes the knife up. But just then his ma scoops up the rifle where he's thrown it and I see her in a kind of haze, tying that torn white petticoat around the barrel. Then starting towards the front door...

72

"I'm going down the hill now, Albie " Ma says.

"Please, Ma,don't go," he tells her..

"Hey boy," I interrupt him. " the pain's
pretty bad!. Flick it out quick and let's get it over with !:

"I'm going down to try to find out who's trying to kill us and why because somebody has got to figure out how to bring an end to this mayhem,once and for all " she says.

"Please don't go, Ma," Albie says. It's like his voice is deepening, as if he's growing taller right in front of me..

"And I'm going alone," his Ma says
because it was my bullet that shot the man bleeding in that chair in front of you..And right now it's him needs your attention more than I do..."

"Please Ma. If you could only wait until.."

"For GOD'S SAKE BOY," I yell. Then all of a sudden a warm weakness comes over me. Then I can't seem to hear anybody talking anymore.

PERCY KETTERING

"It ain't just what I think," Blanding is yelling, half drunk. "It's what's the smartest thing to do is ..."

"I say never mind, every man for himself," Ramos yells. If anything, Ramos is more intoxicated than Blanding. Most of the men are standing around now in front of Blanding's tent – but my word, the stench of stale whiskey after last night's party is enough to make one gag.. Losing so much water, too, — our water reserve has thinned out considerably—since those horses with sacks of water strapped to their bellies—tried to bolt yesterday...And we ought to start promoting some new sources ——perhaps there could be an aquifer somewhere nearby..~......One thing I'm pretty sure about—Those Texans must have brought their own private liquor stash back in Dallas — there's no way I can imagine "Generalissimo" Ridgely ever "officially" signing off on anything like that..

So here we are now, middle of the day, the sun getting hotter , bearing down on this troublesome scene with a remnant of heavy drinkers still tottering about, still coping with what remains of their various hangovers, and the aftermath of that dust storm still littering the landscape. And Ridgley himself meanwhile, over at Mr. Roy's open grave, still mad as a hatter, of course.. "..*noble sacrifice in a great cause,* " he's raving. "*engraved in stone for everlasting glory blah blah blah blah*"

74

But with all these men so bleary-eyed how will I ever get them to listen to what I want to say..?

Because I'm determined to try ! After hearing what Roy started babbling out loud to me on his death bed , ~ I have to say my piece.

"Like it or not," I begin, raising my voice a little, so at least part of those in front of me will start paying attention: "those being blamed and denounced, by Rutherford & Co these days are only what I think you Americans are used to calling "Homesteaders", ~that is, adventurous types trying to cash in on a generous act of Congress which offers them who want it a chance to take their families and themselves and head out West to begin new lives on free land especially set aside for that purpose

"On the train we all rode on not so long ago, you may remember how we listened to angry speeches by the Colonel and the Squire himself and others, denouncing such newcomers and calling them a "pestilence", & congratulating us for being part of a "spontaneous" movement to stamp out their dangerous behavior against those native to this area."

"Right now, I'm ashamed to admit that, at first, I, *myself,* was among those *applauding* such speeches like most of yourselves! What I didn't realize—as maybe some of you *still*

75

don't! —is that what we were hearing was an upside-down inside-out "doctored" version of the truth, by those coveting the land to be awarded oncoming Homesteaders , in which white becomes black, up becomes down, and everyone opposing the fury of Rutherford and friends at not being allowed to keep every inch of Fargos County's land for themselves , somehow turns into a kind of a traiter, in league with Washington Power Brokers and out to deprive our hardworking local ranchers and farmers of their precious freedom to develop every single inch of this County's agricultural land exclusively for *themselves,* in whatever way they see fit !"

"Now as a foreigner, I know it's out of bounds to intrude myself into the Roman Coliseum world of the famous rough and tumble arena of gladiatorial American politics. But surely, in this case, it's about time for someone to step forward, and start telling it like it truly is!"

"Recently I happened to look at a map of the area we're talking about —I mean, the West and mid-West part of the *UNITED* STATES —which still begins with the familiar word, *U N I T E D* , naturally —a word which Webster's Latest Edition informs us, derives from the root word *"unite"*— meaning to *"enter into association, combine forces, come together,"* as in, for instance, *the "quality or action of being*

76

together in feeling, purpose, intent, action, and harmony...etc,"

"On this note, I think it best for me to stop . Let me me thank you, then, for the courtesy of hearing me out. And I also invite any others with questions on their minds, to step forward now, if they're so inclined, and tell us what they are! ..."

When I sit down, there's a long, dramatic pause. I feel a ferocious staring in my own direction. (I must say, my legs began to feel a little wobbly, at this point!, ..)

"What's he getting at," someone finally murmurs. And somebody else asks: "Lies? What's he mean? " And a third: "What kind of lies?" And here's that rogue Blanding coming up to where I'm ready to fade away, his hook manacling my wrist.

"Are you trying to suggest they aint aiming to pay us what they owe us", he asks

" No. But I think all of you could actually be liable for legal action under the law, if you start taking part in raids against newcomers. Especially since chances are, none of the folks on that hit list seem to have had anything to do with Rustling ,either .."..

"Well, I reckon there's plenty of us here done time."
Ramos finally says, and spits once. "But like I say, why don't
we start striking out on our own, wherever we want to go,
and see where it takes us...?"

"Hold-on!" Blanding interrupts.. And then to me:
"Where'd you get all this *so-called inside* information?"

"From young Mr. Roy" I tell him." He began unloading
it all on me on his death bed. He told me the whole thing
was primarily intended as a kind of pro-vo-ca-tion..."

"What's that mean?"

"A sort of a stunt to terrorize various potential
homesteaders out of coming here in the future because the
honorable Squire and his friends have branded them as
obstacles to their own ambitions for expanding their
personal property and grazing grounds... Though, far as I
can tell, there's nothing to fear, on that score, either,
because, as I already said, there's no evidence on record,
far as I can tell, of any Rustling activities attached to any of
those names on your hit list..."

"No Rustling?"

"But they told us, they said we'd all be deputized
later, so we could be–... –"

"Hold on!" Blanding shouts "One minute."

And then we all turn. Because coming down from where all the bodies have been buried in Ridgley's improvised "cemetery," is crazy Genral Whosis himself, with both his guns out, and behind him, trailing along in his dust trail, blindfolded, staggering, and holding onto a gun barrel for a guide is someone else, a stranger.

Here they come between the rows of wasted men, all standing gaping and amazed. Because, my word, it's a woman he's leading. A woman!

RIDGLEY

Oh very clever, very smart!. Coming here, pretending to be some poor victimized traveler, lost or something, and carrying that white flag. Very clever. But when she approaches to our military cemetery, I don't let on at all. Just let her talk and keep her covered.

"Where's the sheriff here?" she cries. "I need to speak to the sheriff."

"Put your rifle down at your feet, Ma am," I tell her.

"But I have to speak to the sheriff!. Because they killed the wrong man, my own husband. The one you want's up there now with my boy, and he's weak, he's wounded. You can take him now without any firing at all."

"Alright. Now turn around. There, take that white cloth, that's it. Now tie it for a blindfold around your head."

"But he's got my son with him," she yells. Aren't you going to do anything about it? Oh I can't believe you're the sheriff — please take me to whoever's in charge..."

"First of all, tie that blindfold, Ma am. Yes, that's it! We can't have anyone spying on our encampment.."

"*Spying?* But that's all dam foolishness, don't you understand? We were coming from Illinois on our way to Buffalo, and we stopped here overnight and..."

"That's right, Ma am. Good and tight. Alright,. Now grab hold of my rifle barrel and start walking."

You see how clever they are!. Making her memorize the same story they told the other one to use! Sending her down here to get us to attack again. It's a fair bet they got the place prepared, as a perfect set-up for an ambush. But if they think I'm going to swallow that, they got another think coming !

So I lead her through that disorderly crowd of men, still reeking with whiskey. Well, let them struggle . Tonight they'll be hollering with thirst again, of course. Which is how troopers learn their trade, of course,—by suffering for their mistakes, ...whenever it's necessary...

Right into my own tent I take her, and sit her down. Take the blind off her too.

"Where's the sheriff," she asks, " take me to the sheriff!"

"I'm his Deputy, Ma am. So whatever you've got on your mind.... ...."

"But you're wasting time ,sitting around down here!. I told you. My son Albie,~ he's only thirteen,~ he's up in that cabin. They shot my husband by mistake, you see and I want to tell it somebody in authority ! But where's the sheriff, why doesn't somebody DO some- thing..."

"Shot your husband, you say ? And was he sort of a short statured man, with a mustache, and slick hair?"

"I told you already. The man owning the cabin is in no condition to fire any more! So why don't you take the opportunity..."

"How many did you say are up at the house, Ma am?"

"I told you already!, Why don't you understand..?, No, I can't believe you're in authority.. Please. take me to somebody *really* in charge!..."

"Sheriff's gone to Claremont, Ma am. So if you've got a personal statement to make..."

"But why don't you run up there yourself, then? He's got my son with him, as I said, but there's nobody else with firearms around ! We were coming from Illinois, and got caught up in all the crazy crossfire going on around here, so why don't you go on up and see for yourselves what I'm talking about... —"

"We can't take any chances, Ma am."

"Chances?"

"How do we know it ain't some kind of an ambush? That you weren't sent down here to lead us into a trap?"

"Ambush! But you must be crazy! I already told you, my husband's been killed for nothing! ..Which has got to be "investigated right away , of course!... I But right now the owner of the cabin himself -no matter whatever *else* he may be wanted for— —has got my boy, trying to help him with— "

"Try not to get too excited, Ma am."

Just the same, I'm not going to hold her here. Because think of it,—sending a woman! Hoping to out-trick us,—having their dirty work done by a woman! Well, it ain't my idea of proper conduct. Using a woman as "bait". That's not proper either for the Military, or any other group of citizens with complaints to make.. ...Still, I have to call her bluff, of course...

82

"Tell you what—you go on back up there, Ma am. We can see the whole front of the place from these rocks ,and we'll be watching to see."

"Watching? To see *what* ?"

"Why the white flag, Maam!. Because you say there's only the three of you up there, and one wounded. So if you and your boy come out and stand in the rise out front with that color waving from a gun barrel, we'll know soon enough everything we need to know.."

"But that Everett's been shot. I shot him a while back,..."

"*You* shot him?"

"I wanted to take my boy, and come down here, and he tried to stop me, so ..."

"Well, all you have to do is *show* us, Ma am. We'll be waiting to see."

Oh you have to give her credit, a real act she's putting on! Telling me it was her shot Everett! And only *three* of them up there – what about all those shots raining on my men yesterday, coming from ghosts were they? Still, you have to give her credit for nerve"–

"Here's the blindfold, Ma am. If you're intending to start back better go now, while it's still light enough to see the color of that flag..."

83

We come out of the tent. Walking right out into a semicircle of eyes, blinking with confusion and roiling with bad feelings. Guns in their hands, and Blanding and Ramos standing tough, and even that Englishman, Kettering, with a funny look on his face.

But I don't let their insubordination get started. Once you show your Command indecision, fear, your command's discipline's gone! And our duty's still lyin before us!".

"Open up," I say, and with that woman in front of me as a kind of shield. "I order you men to let us pass."

"Looks like it ain't clear who's ordering who," someone says.

"Let us pass, Mr. Blanding. I order you -- instruct the men to let us pass..."

"Just seems like I can't do a thing with them anymore, Mr. Ridgley."

"Mr. Ridgley, *Sir*," says young Kettering. "There's some questions they'd like to ask..'"

"I'm the one says what questions ought to be asked,' I tell them. "All of you standing there, get out of the way... "

"Where's the sheriff?" the woman suddenly yells, blindfolded. "I need to speak to the sheriff...."

Whiskey in the air, I can smell it real strong. But still can't see anything. Someone's holding my wrist, and all that ugly kind of talk's still flying around.

But they killed Louis for a rustler, didn't they? So that's what they *must* "officially" be here for!, Otherwise, what'd that sign mean ?... And who are these men yelling with the deputy, why isn't there a sheriff around? Oh Albie, Albie, we never should have started towards Buffalo...

"Whether or not they're rustlers," someone's yelling, and a voice, the deputy's, says, "Let us pass. I promised this lady safe conduct."

"Safe conduct!"

"Get out of the way Blanding..."

"I reckon we'd sort of like to ask her a few questions."

"I said get out of the way..."

"Did you hear that Ramos?"

"I'll count to six, Blanding..."

"In that case, Mr. General Whosis....."

Just then there's a shout. I hear a lot of heavy running, like men in a wild chase. And yelling too. "Look out, the horses. Someone's trying to ride away with the horses..."

Yelling and shouting, a crazy tumult!. And still the blindfold's on my eyes, a hand's got hold of my wrist. And then the deputy's voice says, in what seems to be a temporary silence , "Kettering", I promised this woman safe conduct back up that hill. You're to escort her far as the bend in the gorge. But keep out of sight, they might still start shooting..."

"But Mr. Ridgley, the horses!. If some men are trying to steal..."

"I'll go see about the horses . You escort that woman."

"Shouldn't we both go and see to the..."

"My judgment's made up, Kettering! I told you: escort the woman!....I'll take care of the rest....."

Oh I don't understand!. What's he talking about, where have those others run to? And who's this now grasping my wrist. Thin fingers, another voice entirely. Foreign sounding. And if these men aren't deputies, who are they? But I seen it, I seen the sign they put on Louis, 'afore they shsot him. . "Death to rustlers," it said...

All of a sudden, the blindfold comes off. Here we are at the foot of the gorge. I'm looking into a youngish face, thin, bearded, and with light blond eyebrows.

"Quick Miss, what is it, who sent you, what'd you come to tell Ridgley?"

"Ridgley? I don't know who Ridgley is? Who are you, you're not talking right, either.. Why do they have to put a blindfold on me?"

"Listen, never mind, I can't explain what's happening right now !... But try making believe we're just taking a friendly little walk. And here are some papers, try stuffing them in your clothing, somehow. If he notices, he's liable to start shooting

"*Whose* liable to start shooting ? I have no idea what you're talking about! So~

But he turns and runs off down the slope. There below I can see now, that deputy, or whoever he is, watching us. And something's been shoved in my hand, like a long rolled up sheaf of papers.

Oh Albie, Albie, I don't care who they are. If they'll only get us away from here! So please, make him do like I say this time, God.

Please. Please.

"What happened, boy?"

"You sort of fainted, Mr. Everett."

"You get the bullet out?"

"Yes sir. But you lost blood when I was trying to do it..."

"Who tied that bandage on?"

"It was me did it, Mr. Everett. I used that pair of pajamas was hanging in that other room..."

Then I look around. The room's empty, save for the two of us. Blood is streaking the floor, and outside the shadows are longer over the hills. That must mean it's getting along towards sundown. But how long was I out?

"Where's your Ma, boy?"

"She's...she went off, Mr. Everett... I couldn't stop her from going..."

"That was a foolish thing to do, boy...If she tells them it's only three of us up here, and one of them herself...oh that was crazy foolishness, boy."

"Yes Sir...but she wouldn't listen to me, sir.. ... I told her it weren't true..."

"*What* weren't true, boy?"

88

"That you're a..."

"Cattle thief?"

"Yes Sir."

"Why ain't you ready to believe it, boy?"

"You just ain't, that' all..."

Who was it said children and animals 're truer in sniffing what's wrong about people than anyone else. I don't know. Maybe that ain't entirely talk. Because here's this boy, don't know me more'n twenty-four hours! And look what he done.

"Is it Indians, Mr. Everett?"

"What's that, boy?"

"Shooting at us from down the valley? Is it Indians? Because Ma went down by herself, and I was thinking if you're alright, maybe I ought to..."

"It ain't Indians, boy, but that was nothing for her to do. I told you, she shouldn't have gone. Anyway, no use in thinking about that right now. Only I ain't going to stop you if you want to make a break yourself..."

"Sir?"

"See out this side window. Now you look careful...There, where that hill begins, right about a third from the bottom. You see about three feet from the end of the shale wall...

"Yes Sir."

"You push through there, there's a hole about big enough for a small man to crawl through, maybe ten, fifteen feet. Then it widens out, sort of a cavern. Goes clear through that hill and comes out on the north side maybe three quarters of a mile away. High up where those hills begin...so by following a compass...you know how to read a hand compass, boy?"

"No Sir..."

"Ain't nothin' difficult to learn. By following it you could go the fifteen or twenty miles to the Buffalo road, though it's probably all dusted over right now. What do you think, boy...?"

"I ain't going to go off without her coming...and not leaving you here, either..."

"Never mind about me, boy. And as for your Ma..."

"Mr. Everett, look!"

It's her!. And all alone. Climbing that hill as if she was taking a stroll, and not a soul with her.

"Maybe that means they're gone, and everything'll be all right now. So I'm going to..."

"Wait a second, boy. Close that door. We're not going to open it till she comes within hollering range."

We stand there, waiting. Sweat all over me, that sun going down. But anyway, one good thing, the bullet's out, he got it out clean!. Not that I feel so good, but far as infection goes, things're looking better.. maybe it's my turn for a little bit of luck... But now that woman's running right up close, and comes into the room, dazed and sort of hysterical.

"Albie, Albie..."

"What is it, who was it Ma?...what happened, who's down there?"

"Oh they blindfolded me, Albie!, They made me walk with cloth over my eyes! And that deputy told me to get us two out in front to the house with a bed sheet for a sign, and wouldn't any harm come to you."

"Deputy...what're you talking about...?"

"I didn't see a man, except him, and that foreigner. Oh it's all mixed up, but I know they mean to get in here, they mean to kill him, and we got to stand out and take that bed sheet and..."

"Here, sit down a minute Ma. You ain't makin' sense, is she Mr. Everett?"

"What's she carrying in her hand, boy?"

He gives it to me. I'm still weak, sitting there all the while, & she talking away, him trying to understand her. But when I open what she's been carrying, a little book falls out, just a pad and a lot of drawing on it.

A lot of drawing!.

Why it's Rutherford himself, and here's the young heir himself, too! And this one shows that damn puffed up bastard of a so-called "*Colonel*," --Samson is his name,-- with acreage next to Rutherford south of Claremont. And look at this -- unloading rifles from what looks like a train or a caboose or something! And who are these men, they don't look like locals to me.

Oh but the whole thing's plain!. That crazy squirel. Must've gone plain out of his cranium.. But who give these sketches to her, what happened down there...?

"Albie, Albie..."

"Get a hold of yourself now, Ma. It's all right. I'm not even scratched, see...?"

"They put a blindfold on me, Albie. I could smell the whiskey, and..."

"Please start at the beginning, Ma. Tell us what happened..."

Crack, crack, crack!. We hear a sudden volley of shots in that fading light. But it comes from way down, it ain't moving up in this direction. And now silence.

"While it's still light," that woman's babbling away. "Please, Albie. We got to get that sheet and stand out in front like he said. Otherwise..."

"When *who* said? Please, try to stop crying for a second, Ma am and tell us...what's *really* happening down there "

She looks at me, tears streaking her face, that boy holding her elbow. Then she recoils. She backs up.

"Don't you come near me, you rotten cattle thief." she says.

HOOK

I'm thirty-seven years old, I been in trouble since my hand come off when I was a kid back in Wyoming twenty-five years ago. Been to fourteen states, shipped to the Caribbean, been run out of half a dozen counties in the southwest, Mexico too. And I seen a lot of cruel bastards in my time, a lot of them, learning me it ain't Christian verses that makes the world go round.

But I ain't never seen anyone like *him*!. Never!. Ain't just him shooting and that cold face of his, but there's something unstrung in his head. Know what I mean? Like as

93

if he *enjoyed* shooting them two boys we caught trying to sneak off with horses, though the others got away from him at that. But holding a court trial the way he did?, And I swear I still don't know how it happened!. We were all drunk, everyone was against him, and all he did was talk, his hands on his guns. All he did was make a goddam speech, and afterwards shoot those two boys himself, carrying out the verdict of the military court, he says. No one answering a word.

That Ridgley's a madman!. But not so mad he don't know this country, not so crazy he don't know how to lead us out of here back to Claremont if he wanted. But he won't, he won't do it until he climbs that hill again and gets us all killed in tryin!'.

I don't know whether he was lying about the woman. "A spy," he said. "Sent to make us think wasn't anyone up there but Everett and a kid and herself." Everyone standing around not knowing what to think and that madman's mouth going and going. "So we'll see, men," he says. "Because I told her to put a white sheet out if it was okay, and to have them both come in front and stand on the porch..."

Well, we aint seen anybody with any white sheet, and it's getting' dark now.. No use to stand waiting any longer.

But the crazy thing is even though the man's out of his brain, all his reasons ain't so crazy. "We got to get water," he says. "You want to go on drinking that whisky, I ain't gonna order you to stop. But the ration'll be gone by tomorrow...and then what'll happen—you'll go crazy, your insides'll be fired, your tongues will start festering. And any man driving off has a day's ride 'for he gets to where water is. Even if he knew where to head for..."

Sitting there listening to him, no one makes a move to shoot the little bastard. Eight of us left out of fifteen, not counting that foreigner, and all because we got a lunatic here, and ain't no one with the guts to shoot him down.

Here's the Englishman, whatever his name is, talking to Billy McKensie. Saying we'll all be arrested and taken into custody because they ain't no rustlers up there, a lot of that kind of talk. Well who cares! All I want is to get the hell out of here!...Still, Ridgley's right about water, though I reckon I'm ready to take a chance on headin' for the main road, Indians or no Indians! And with all the money shared from those casualties, we'd could be sitting pretty. Because we could concoct a story no one could prove wrong!.. Only we got to get rid of that crazy man first, no telling what he's liable to do next. Sure, I'm willing for a try to get water from that well on the west side tomorrow, but it's Ridgley we got to stop first.

Then I call that foreigner over. I talk to him.

"I seen you whispering with the General," I ask. "What'd he want?"

"Why…" he says. He looks at me. His look ain't giving me nothing.

"Not that I care," I tell him. "But there's nobody'd here able to guarantee you might not run into some sort of unfortunate "accident" way out here , Kettering. And you a foreigner and all…"

"Is that a threat, Blanding?"

"What was you and Ridgley jawing about?"

"Why…" Kettering says. "He wants me to draw him, that's all."

"*Draw* him! When?"

"Tonight…it's to help him keep awake, though he didn't say it. But I'm sure that's the reason."

"All right, that's fine. That fits in with our plans just fine. Now listen to me, Kettering…"

I begin talking to him, fast, and without any words lost. He ain't letting me see what he thinks and I ain't making out as if I care. Then I finish and he looks at me. He stares at Ramos and McKensie and the rest. Then he nods.

"How long has it been, "Ridgley is asking me, "since you've been in London, Mr. Kettering?"

"About two years," I tell him. For the last half hour we've been here in this tent, and my word, has it only been four days since that trainful of transplanted Texans stopped in the middle of that ranchland. But so much has happened since then—so many poor chaps killed, and this bloody idiot with Colonel Samson's hat still on, terrorizing all of us here in the middle of the Lord knows where.

Well all my life I've been a bloody fraud, yes why not admit it. Full of restlessness, fancying myself a bit of a swashbuckler and all that. Came all the way here to the States for the reason, although the family couldn't afford the ruddy fees, if truth be known. Because what does it mean really? That I'm only a bloody coward inside!. Yes and here's a clear cut case,- a chap knows what he should do and he can't do anything, only think how frightful the whole thing is, and not do one bloody thing!.

"Travel," Ridgley is telling me. "That's what I hoped for. But doctors vetoed me, it was doctors told me I had only a few months to live, do you believe that Kettering? Yes, they kept me from being what I was destined to

97

become. Oh but you can ruin your life if you keep on following the warnings of timid men. Never do it, Kettering, the thing to do is follow your own bent, great men have their own destiny. What do prescriptions matter?"

Wild and by the light of those suspended candles, he looks like a wraith of some kind. How long since the blighter's slept? But suddenly thinking of those others, Blanding and his ilk, I get an idea.

"Mr. Ridgley, listen..."

After I tell him, he doesn't move for a second. His eyes show a peculiar light, you might think the crazy fellow's actually happy to hear men are planning to kill him. Then he moves with speed. The next thing I know he has taken a few pillows, and some string, and propped the whole thing up in the very chair he'd been sitting in, and is crouched down behind the gun chest in the rear of the tent, his pistols ready.

"Go right on sketching, Mr. Kettering," he said. "And don't stop talking either. Let them think you're talking to me."

"Talking? To myself?"

"It doesn't matter what you say, so long as they hear your voice. Because they'll think it's you talking and myself listening. Yes, I think that shadow in the chair should be satisfactory..."

What I hoped was they'd shoot each other. That he would go and search Blanding out and then perhaps we could be rid of these two at least, so I might have a chance to persuade a few of the others. But I didn't expect him to play possum. Well, I wasn't cut out for this sort of thing. There's the chair, in silhouette against the tent as I promised Blanding, and here I am, standing exposed between what could easily be turned into a crossfire.

I'm so parched too, so thirsty. But if we don't get some water pretty soon, we'll have to do something drastic. That sun must get to a hundred and twenty degrees in the afternoon. And all the time I'm trying to keep my mind from dwelling on those two crazy blighters crawling towards us now, and those poor devils up there on the hill, and that woman, whoever she was. Because any second now—any second there's going to be a crossfire, and oh Lord, oh Lord, how am I going to get out of all this and back to where I shouldn't have left in the first place. Because why not admit it, I'm terrified, babbling away like a ninny about London and tourists and...

"Don't stop!" Ridgley orders from in darkness behind that chest. "Keep on talking away now, Kettering..."

"The...Nottingham cathedral is...of course...one of the most interesting things to...see...and..."

"That's it. Keep on talking."

MRS. AMY FINLETTER

I hardly recognize him for my own son anymore! Because it seems like years instead of days that we drove up this hill with that sick horse, asking for a night's bedding. And Albie ain't the same,— everything's made him see like he was suddenly grown, instead of only going on fourteen!, But I still can't stand it when they start whispering, keeping me from hearing what they don't want me to hear. What was it he told Albie just then? And now that boy going off by himself, carrying those buckets, and him following, too, with a bag full of salt...to get us water, he said. And telling me to fire if anyone comes.

I don't know, I don't know. Could that be the truth he told before? About how those sketches showed it wasn't deputies at all in the valley, but a gang of marauding hired hands sent by some old Squire, I forget his name, to see

100

there ain't but one man says how much acreage is used and where in this county.

Then that'd mean they murdered my Louis for nothing. But why would anybody do that ?, He weren't a man to take offense at somebody else's law breaking?. And all that whisky I smelled down there, and that deputy talking like he did ?.. Whoever he was...just the same, he didn't give me no reason to accuse him except maybe that blindfold he put on. And what about that foreigner? Oh it's too much for a stranger to try to take in altogether...

Still, that sign said *"death to rustlers"*, I saw it plain. And that little man down there was wearing a uniform of some kind, yes he braid on on both shoulders.. So he must have been an official, doesn't that sound logical? Well, I could go out now and wave that torn petticoat. Could take that rifle and attach my petticoat to it and fire a few times. Because if they're still looking up here like he says, if it ain't still too dark yet...

Hello, here's a notebook on the floor, it must have fallen from Everett's pocket. What's he writing down all the time? Dates and happenings it looks like, yes that's all it is, only a diary... And here's an entry made only a month ago... "April 24. – Hoed the west field. Julia helped though I told her not to come out, even though she's only a few months gone, it ain't right work for her to do. And Larry romping and hollering all over the place, such a pest for a five year old...Well, we sure hope he gets himself a sis this time, that's what Julia wants, and I'm getting used to the idea myself. But sitting there, the three of us eating lunch outdoors, and looking over these fields we built up ourselves in less than two years after homesteading out here from Ohio, something wonderful came over me. Seems like there ain't nothing a man isn't king over, when he's sitting on his own land......

"April 30. Visit from my Cy Muller. Talk about the fracas out at Henry Williams place. Bunch of troublemakers come over, they couldn't tell if it was Emerson sent them, or Rutherford, but it was one of those troublemaking ranchers, they were sniping at his fence, and pulling up his corn when he caught them. Rode away yelling threats and cuss words. I told them we got to do something to defend ourselves, it ain't only us they're trying to scare off, it's others coming after. And who's going to be safe if you can't stand behind the protection of the laws......

"May 4. This morning found twelve sheep slaughtered in the south pasture. No traces of anything, but I didn't tell Julia. Why worry her? Only after everything this last year, – drought, and that hoof disease and me spraining my knee like I did, seems like now we got the worse craziness of all to deal with. But I don't care, let 'em say what they want. This is my land......

"May 8. Can't write much today. Julia and the boy both took sick sudden-like with what they call plains fever. Had Doc Hodgins over from Buffalo. He ain't told me anything definite yet......

"May 9. Both of them worse. They boy ain't said a word for a whole day. Oh I don't know what this should have come to me, why should everything be put on one man? I got to pray......

"May 10. 2:45 A.M. Larry ain't breathing. I just looked in at him... but thank God, Julia's took too feverish herself right now to know.....

6 A.M. Julia passed away.....

"May 12. Buried my wife and boy in the north pasturage on a hill overlooking the barley. Didn't do nothing all day but sit there. Don't seem like I want to do anything at all anymore, just stay where they are......"

No use to read anymore, my eyes are all misted up. But how could he be any thief, not if he's the one writ those pages!... And the way he went around here, so sullen and bad tempered, anyone just listening to him wouldn't have thought...

"Ma," Albie says. "We did it. We fixed 'em!."

"Close the door, boy," Everett tells him, and don't look at me at all. Both of them with heavy buckets of water, and splashing all around.

"We salted the well, Ma. Because Mr. Everett said...."

"You be quiet now, boy. Your Ma ain't interested in what we're doing to those as she considers rightful in their actions......"

He looks pale. Just goes and sits down and it hurts him to move around, you can see that, his shoulder's paining him again. And here's Albie jumping and jumping like a possum after a squirrel.

"We did it Ma! We put salt in the well! Because Mr. Everett says they'll be coming for water most likely, soon, and he ain't going to leave them no supply. I took the sack and held it over, and...."

"That's enough boy," Mr. Everett says.
"you talk like a goose cackling. Your ma don't want to hear nothing about it."

"He said you'd be gone afore we got back, and taken those extra guns with you. But I knew you wouldn't I said how wrong he was. Because you know he's right now, don't you Ma? Don't you?"

"Boy," Everett shouts from his corner. "Be quiet!. You hear me?"

Then he don't say anything. Albie shuts up, goes to sit at the window. It's dark out. We can see the light from those campfires shining from the valley.

HOOK

That dirty doublecrossing foreigner!.

Oh I'll get to him. I'll wait for the right time and get to him !. Because he must have spilled it, he got Ridgley to rig those damn pillows in a chair, waiting for us like a dirty rattlesnake. Shooting through the canvas like that and us not knowing what happened, and that limey bastard squealing inside like a stuck pig, though he probably weren't hurt bad at all, he'd be just lucky enough to get nicked...

Only one blooded was *me*, my damn wrist!. So now here we are in this damn tent, and Ramos blaming me, sayin' it's my fault, I shouldn't have trusted that Englishman. How'd I know he was ready to give everything away? And them two in Ridgley's tent, waiting for daybreak, and Ridgley with a whole case full of ammunition, and us with only enough bullets left to blow our own brains out.

But I told them, I said it was then or never. Rush the tent, kill him, kill the 'little crazy madman afore he kills us. Now they think he's some kind of superman, and him with all that ammunition in his luggage chest. But he got to sleep sometime, he ain't gonna stay awake forever, he's no more'n a single man, outnumbered five times over.

Only now I got to use my head. This lousy hook's right now no use, and my other wrist's bloody from that one lucky shot. I got McKensy to bandage it but it still pains like hell's devils. Well, tomorrow we'll see what happens. No one can get at those horses now either, long as he stays where he is, and that case of ammunition next to him, and that dirty double-crossing limey bastard in there, bowing and crawling.

I'll get him for what he done! My wrist torn bloody and that king popinjay sitting on a case of cartridges, but I'll cut them both to pieces if it's all I ever do!. I swear it!.

COREY EVERTT

Must have fallen asleep. Slumped against that window, and that rifle jogging my shoulder. But what time is it, some time after midnight? And something boiling, soup or something, and that fireplace lit with a

106

new flame, and Albie nowhere to be seen.

"Albie, Albie....."

"You slept three hours," the woman says. She's standing by that pot and with that rifle of hers strung across the back by the same cloth served her before as a flag. She shouldn't use up our water for soup like she's doing. But just the same something's changed on her face.

"Where's Albie..."

"He's gone," she says. " I sent him off."

"You sent him...?

"He had to borrow your compass, "she says, stirring that pot. "I showed him how to use it the way you told But I sent him away before sun up , because if he was going to wait any longer, the light might come up too strong..."

"You mean you explained what's been happening to us ..."

"Wasn't the best note I wrote., But I hope everyone'll get to understand what we've been going through since we stayed over at your place.. Not that I knew who to address it. Just the sheriff, Buffalo. Was that alright?"

I don't say anything. My shoulder's beginning again, and that beating pulse in my forehead which means maybe it's going to start once more. But all I can think of is: _she sent that boy off._ A stranger to me, and him her whole life and it's over 20 miles to the main road alone, even if he gets through the cave and all. But she did it!. Wrote the note, sent him off!. And here it was, not six hours ago in this very same room she made all that racket, ending up by spitting like a cat from rage. And now tells me so calm it's hard to believe that she sent him off …

Or maybe she didn't. She might have talked that boy into doing something *else*. Because she's his Ma, even if he's rare grown up boy, And if she had all this time to talk to him, to persuade him…

"You want some soup?" the woman asks.

I turn to look at her. By the light of that fire, that rifle slung on to her shoulders, and all that weak womanly weepiness gone out of her for the moment, why she looks like the queer spittin' image of Albie himself. Mouth in a thin line. Eyes set as cut amethyst. Handing me a plate of soup and something else along with it.

"Found this on the floor, " she says. "Belongs to you by the name writ on the cover."

She hands me my diary. Her eyes on mine, her hand touching the end of the book, touching my own fingers as she hands it over. Then she turns away, stirs the soup. I go to the window, take the rifle up. My shoulder's beginning to hurt again. But all I can think of is – strangers to me and she sent him, she sent that boy alone and through hill country filled with coyotes she don't know nothing about, and maybe Indians too, and ten miles to the road at least...

"Getting light soon," she says, by the hanging pots.

We look at each other. Both of us are thinking the same thing, and I decide to encourage her a piece.

"That's some boy," I say. "Ain't nothing usual going to faze him from getting to that road. And if he gets a good start before the heat sets in..."

But I ain't so sure. I know how far he's got to go. And through what. So if praying is any use, I ain't going to ignore it.

Then I hear a sound of lips whispering. It's her. She's doing it for both of us.

THIRD DAY

Going to be hot as yesterday, sun's already eighty or over. But if I yell, those men can still hear what I'm saying, Sure, there's not more than fifty yards between this tent and theirs. Blandings got 'em all worked up against me, probably. Well never mind, they'll come around. To keep command, you've got to act in command! We came here to do our duty, bound and sworn to before the Squire himself! And as that duty fell on *me*, I'm not going to let it fall by the wayside... But troops have to be pushed as well as led. I've been explaining that to Kettering all night, it was lucky that he was here with me. Over two days without sleep – left alone, I might not have been able to keep it up. But I *did*. Well it takes crisis to bring out the authentic qualities in a man.

"Kettering," I say, "Kettering..."

He looks at me. His lips are cracked. Oh no, that face isn't the amused foreigner any more I.

"What is your opinion, Kettering?"

"What?"

"We are having a conference. I order you to transcribe notes, take down these deliberations..."

"Take down?" You mean transcribe—but for God's sakes…, Ridgley—"

"*Mister* Ridgley, Sir !

"I don't care what the bloody hell you call yourself!. You're a bloody butcher, that's what you are!. Driving us all to hell here, and those poor innocent chaps on the hill…"

"Control yourself, Kettering!. I order you to get a grip on yourself…do you hear me?"

Oh but he's too weak, listen to him, all sighs and regrets and whatnot.. like a woman. What did these men come out here *for* if they can't expect to stand up under fire?. Full of pretensions, but here comes a crisis, and I appoint him an officer to my staff and what does he do? – Crouches like a pig, squealing and squalling!….

"Kettering…KETTERING!"

No, it's no good. He just crouches there. Well let him alone for a while, he'll come around. Then I go to the door of my tent.

"Blanding…BLANDING!"

No answer. But I know they can't get a good shot in this direction. Besides, all this gear's here to hide behind, and our vantage's ten times better. That's why I choose this site for the Colonel to begin from..Audacity means nothing without the quality of surprise to go with it.

"Can you hear me Blanding?..I want you all to pay attention"

Still not a sound. But there's no need for me to yell even.

"I have thought of what's needed to do to accomplish our mission here. And at the same time get us out of our difficulties. So you have my oath as Commander: I'll put the questions up to majority vote. We can go on to Buffalo or return to Claremont. But we can't do either without horses, water, and knowledge of the way. The last is no problem, since I am on home ground. But for the first we need access to that high ground, and the supplies they have up there. So if you're willing to submit to proper discipline..."

Hello, they're shooting at me!. Well, let them waste their bullets, I know how much they have.

"Kettering..Kettering!"

My God, talk about weaklings...

"Stand up Kettering. On your feet now...

"Bloody butcher of a..."

"Stop that...STOP THAT!"

No, I didn't mean to yell. Control, keep control at all times. But we still have this gallon jug of water, it was packed in with those boards and tins. Can't use much, need it as barter. But perhaps a pinch...

"Get up Kettering...we have a ration of water coming to us..."

"Water..."

"On your feet...Here, we may have to bargain with this jug. Don't spill that cup."

Disgusting weakling!. But no, I mustn't drink too fast. Easy, that's it. And suddenly we hear commotion outside. I lift up the flap two inches. There milling around in front of their tent are McKensy and Baring and Ramos all fighting together, and someone's yelling at them, it's Blanding's voice. But what are those pails tipped over on the ground, where did that water come from?"

"Blanding." I yell. "Listen to me. Blanding..."

HOOK

Ramos and me and McKensy and Baring and the Mexican Alvirez are still breathing heavy, and those men's mouths still wet with that sickening salt water they were trying to drink. But I talk to them. I try to get them to listen to me.

"You all must be crazy!. Because I told you something wasn't right – letting us get that easy right up to the well and almost in daylight, why they could have fired on us from the house if they wanted, we were within range. But they let us fill those buckets, they let us bring them on down without one shot. So do you know what'd happen if I hadn't kicked 'em over – you'd all've got to fighting about whether or not you was going to go crazy from the salt taste or not. Because that's what it does, drives you crazy out of your heads!. And Ridgley over there with his ammunition, and that damn Englishman toadying him..."

"We need water," Baring says, and Alvirez, the Mexican is muttering in Spanish, "Holy Mother of God... Holy Mother of God."

Ramos looks at me doubtfully. It ain't a pretty situation. Seven men crowded into this tent, and everyone half crazy from heat and thirst and fear.

"Listen, I say. "Ain't no one risking himself on that fool house anymore. But you know Ridgley's out of his head! And with that ammunition he's got – you know our bullets ain't going to last long.

"*Ridgley!*" Alvirez says. He's short, about five—seven , and with eyes restless as scorpions. Straight black hair and scorpion eyes. *"Ridgley..."* And gets up suddenly and takes his rifle and goes to the tent opening.

"Where you going...come back here..."

"Hijo de Vacal."

"Alvirez!" Ramos yells and cocks his own rifle.

But I stop him. Because we don't have hardly a few dozen rounds left among us and we can't waste them like that. And the next thing we know Alvirez is gone.

Swearing in Spanish he is, loud, and walking across that flat space to where that senseless bastard is crouched in his tent. We hear Ridgley yelling at him to stop where he is and don't take no further step.

Then a shot. Just one. Then Ridgley's voice again.

"I told him, I warned him!...Nothing's going to be done that way, remember I have the bullets...Are you there, Blanding?"

We don't say a thing. Six of us left now, and the rest gone, either deserted or murdered by him and his mad play-acting and attacks on that house. But then after a few minutes, Ridgley calls out again.

"I've got a jug of water here...Blanding, do you hear?...There was a jug of water packed in the tool chest...Kettering's going to bring a cupful thirty yards to the center of the clearing and I've got my rifle aimed. So if I I'm going." McKensy says.

"Ramos, keep him from..."

"No." Ramos says. "Let him go. If he really has some water..."

"It's probably a trick. How do we know that..."

"No. Go ahead, McKensy."

"Can you hear me, Blanding?" Ridgley's yelling.

That poor devil Alvirez's groaning in Spanish, probably bleeding to death out there, but my wrist's too numb now, and McKensy's walking out through the flap and Ramos training his gun on me for safe keeping.

"Go ahead, Mac," Ramos says. "We gotta take a chance..."

COREY EVERETT

"Not that I want to keep bothering about it," the woman repeats for the sixth time, "but how long did you say it would be before he gets to Buffalo?"

"That depends on where he got a ride on the road, Ma'am. We can't tell how many miles he'll have to walk."

118

"But you said before you weren't doubtful, you told me..."

"I said *maybe*, Ma'am. Ain't no use in trying to fool ourselves."

"Oh I wish I'd a gone instead! Maybe I should've tried myself before I..."

"That wouldn't a done no good, Ma'am. First place, ain't nobody but a small boy could have got through that cave. And then that son of yours is wiry. I ain't losing hope."

"Hope! Why before you said you were confident!"

"I *am* confident, Ma'am. Hopeful and confident is what I am. Now if you're not too tired, this box could stand more dirt."

She goes down to the cellar again, carrying that empty bucket. My shoulder's throbbing, weakness coming and going. Well I don't know. Maybe this whole plan is crazy anyway. Because here I am trying to fix a broken stovepipe into a regular mortar piece, and with just this empty box as a anchor. But if we fill it with dirt, if we stick that pipe in deep, and pack it close, maybe it'll work. Because there ain't many bullets left to do damage if they come at us again, and since I got those few old mortar shells we found last winter in the west pasture.....Lucky for me that regiment from Ft. McKinney used to maneuver this neighborhood,

119

though those shells are real corroded. Maybe they won't even work. And they might even explode the wrong way, killing us both in here without anyone else having to lift a finger. Just the same, I have to pretend I know what I'm doing, because she's worried enough about her boy. Which is no more'n I am myself.

"That's fine, Ma'am, fine," I say when she comes up again, sweating and panting, and that bucket full of dirt. Then she sits down, puts a hand over her face. She's all fatigued. But even so, sitting there and drooping, she ain't complaining any more.

"It's all my fault," she says, and looks at the floor.

"Ma'am?"

"It was only me that wanted to come out here to Arizona!" she says. "All my friends in Illinois kept telling us it was crazy, and Albie with all his friends back there in school, even if his father wasn't anything more than a drunk and a no good to boot."

I look away. Her voice comes in loud, then soft. My forehead's sizzling again.

"Without me wanting it so, we wouldn't be here, and that was a dream I had for all last winter," she goes on, talking more to the floor boards than to any listening ear. "Because I wanted a good life for him, not where

120

everyone'd be able to point out who his Pa was and laugh in his face when he growed up a little. Yes that's what they'd be doin' if we stayed. And Albie's like me, he don't take after that Finletter at all."

I don't say anything. But as if she might have heard me wondering the craziness of a woman like her marrying a man like *that*, she goes on, brooding the whole thing out.

"Thirty-three years old is what I am, I don't mind saying it! And I never was anything to rave over, what's the use of telling different. But that don't mean I was fixing to stay all my days in Marion, New York, which is where everyone's got his head buried ten feet deep in the same things their grandfathers did, and them doing it no better, or maybe even worse."

"If you're rested, Ma'am?" I say. Because I don't want to hear what she's likely to tell. Some things, you hear them, and nothing can ever take them back.

"Dental surgeon and specialist is what he called himself in those days, and all those fancy stickers on that suitcase of his. But he wasn't so loud then, and I was dumber than most. He wasn't no more studied for teeth than I am for gizzards!. But he knew how to get his satisfaction, and without even promises. So two months tracing was what it took me to find out all the places he'd been kicked out of even, and me carrying that boy in me all the time."

"If you're rested, Ma'am," I begin, and look at that empty pail.

"All I care about is Albie," she says, rocking sort of back and forth. "All I want's his proper growth, and seeing that bad blood which wasn't his fault beaten out of him, and something good happen for him later on in a place where people won't be liable to nudge and elbow one another. I hoped that out here in all the new territory Finletter might change some., And if he didn't of his own account, folks might *make* him. And then Albie might be able…one day…to…"

She stops. Out of breath. Or caught up in worry, I don't know which. But then I realize what she probably needs is something else to talk about. So I groan a little. I turn my head. I nod toward that bandage.

"Bleeding again, Ma'am." Then she takes a few steps. "You'll find clothing to wear in that other room."

But the fact is, I'm not entirely lying. Because it seems like a year since I felt my proper strength, and here we are now with that stove pipe mortar and those ancient shells, and that boy off in the hills somewhere.

When I sigh again, I don't know if it's from really feeling weak, or feeling plain sorry for all of us.

<u>ALBIE FINLETTER</u>

Look at all those wagons and blankets!. But the men don't seem friendly to me, ain't hardly any of them smiling. Babies on the women's backs, too, just like the pictures I seen of Indians once. But they've been passing by for maybe half an hour already, where are they headed for, wonder how they're called?

Oh I'd like to ask them for water. And a horse too, yes maybe they're friendly to people in these parts. But I don't dare do it. Suppose they ain't what I think? And Ma and Mr. Everett back in that house. No, I don't dare show myself. Oh but it ain't maybe a hundred yards between us now and if I make a break for those other bushes over there, will they see me?

Well, I gotta try it, got to take a chance. Because the road's where all the traffic is, Mr. Everett said so. And it ain't but less than twenty miles to Buffalo, goin' that way, though this country around here is all up and down, my feet ain't gonna last long stayin' in these hills.

Come on, gotta make a run for it!. Cause Ma's back in that house with, Mr. Everett, and that bunch of crazy robbers down below!. Count to three, that's what I'll do, then make a run for the other side.

Alright. Ready?

One. Two. THREE......

HOOK

Crazy fools! Dig, dig, dig – go ahead, you won't find any water over there! But all right, I don't care. It ain't my concern. If you want to listen to that crazy madman again after everything that's happened, and just because he pretends to know where you'll find water...you'll see how much he knows.

Look at him, -his eyes ain't human!. How much longer is he going to keep it up? He ain't had no sleep in three days, and no one ain't even seen him yawn. Walking around, telling us where to put our spades, – you don't see him digging himself, do you? Not till hell freezes he won't.

But I got to think ahead. Two horses left, and six men, and if they don't find water those horses ain't going to last long, either. What if I break towards that house? But that'd mean explaining how I came to be here *myself*, giving up all that we've got so far, too. No, that don't seem like anything

124

clever. What I got to do, I got to figure out a way to get rid of them,- and with someone else to help,- because my wrist being shot and all – I couldn't do much riding off alone. But first thing is to kill Ridgley, get rid of Ridgley!. That's project Number one!, - Him and that sniveling Englishman walking around in his shadow! Oh how I hate that double-crossing foreigner! Because if he didn't do that, sneak on us, our crazy Make Believe General'd be rotting right now, and the rest of us might have had some kind of...

Wait a minute, wasn't Kettering always so quick to be drawing everybody before, saying that's what he come for? And what's to become of all those drawings?..Everyone's face on them plain as daylight !. Who's to say he ain't above selling them to the wrong party? I ain't sayin' he's ever gonna get the chance but just supposing something happens and he *is*?

Then I force myself. I walk over to the two of them, one tall and quaking, the other short, and still giving that cocky strut of his, as if God himself had better stand stiff when he comes by.

Kettering don't say anything to me, but Ridgley's full of talk how it's better to be reasonable, and how he's glad I've turned out sensible and so on. Then I tell them both.

"What about his drawings?"

"Drawings?"

"If he's so goddam *un*interested, where are our faces he put on paper? Because I don't aim to have this party stuck on no wall, even if we do walk out of here, and..."

"All right, Blanding," Ridgley says, and looks at Kettering.

"With everything's that happened, and good Lord, he talks about drawings as if they were impor..."

"Where *are* they?" I ask, and look at him straight.

"They're in my pack, in the tent, but good Lord..."

"I think it might be a good idea anyway," says Ridgley, "if you was to bring them to me. Just for safekeeping," he says.

Kettering looks at us. Ridgley hasn't moved. All around those others are digging away.

Then Kettering goes off, white and livid. And suddenly he begins running: tears like mad off the clearing, making for that gorge. The next thing I hear, Ridgley's commanding everybody to get clear, give him a clear shot.

Maybe it's because of no sleep and no water or just the strain. But Mr. Superman for once has to use his whole clip. And he misses a few times too. Which ain't to say that he still don't bring that sneak down just the same right before he gets to that bend in the trail where the two big rocks come together. And then Ridgley shouts to all the men who come running.

"I owe you an apology, men!... Yes, a grave apology. Because he *tricked* me, I trusted him as an officer, and he tricked me!."

Beards, staring eyes, panting mouths and wild looks. And Ridgley with those everlasting two guns in his hands, yelling to us.

"He must have given them to her, men, though I was sure nothing passed between them. Yes, my fault, I owe you an apology..."

"You mean they got those pictures up in that house?"

"We have no choice, men. Don't you see? Not only because our duty demands it, and everything we need's in that barn we can't get at behind their enclosure, but they have the *proof*, if he gave them those sketches, it's absolutely necessary that..."

"No!"

I turn, breathing fast. Ramos and McKensy have come up once more, all of them carrying spades, and now it's McKensy talking out, his red hair burned black almost from the sun.

"We ain't risking any more bullets at us," he says. "No one's going to go riding up that slot to be shot down like clay pigeons. All of us dying here for water and..."

"But I've got a plan," Ridgley says. "No one likes to see undue casualties more than myself, but this plan'll work. If you'll listen to me~."

"Plan!," yells Ramos, and spits out once.

"Listen to you!" My voice is yelling, hoarse. "We're in this mess because of *you*. Diggin' with our last strength for water because you and that crazy nut are trying to tell us that..."

"Look," someone cries. Look!"

Old Abe Williams. He hasn't stopped digging once. And now he rushes up and throws a handful of wet slimey mud on the ground right in front of everybody.

"Wet as Texas dew. There's water below that. Come on, don't stand here talking. Come on..."

Everybody scatters. Digging away. Over by the gorge on his back, that Englishman's making his last flutters. And here's Ridgley reloading that clip, triumph spread like dirt all over his face.

A plan? He isn't the only one got a plan. You goddamn popinjay, I'll get you yet!

Lord, Lord, everything's so bright on the quay. I say, glad the family could come to see me off, blamed decent. Not that I expected the old man, anyway. But what has he got against me going to the States so much? I can still hear him, full of shrill complaining about the expense. And if I stay – my whole life spent listening to the insufferable chatter of clerks? But now it's so dark, everything's suddenly so dark, where did they all go...

Odd, so bright and the next minute darker than dreams. I say, where'd everybody go? Am I in hospital? If I could only see something definite, raise my head...

No, I remember, he shot me!. That redness comes from me, it's my own blood !. Because of that Madman, – that goddam bloody *certifiable* madman, and he shot me in cold blood, like all the others, I just couldn't get to that house, and that's why—...

Governor, governor! Help, my wrists, I'm weak, the sun hurts, what are those monstrous colors? Like a bloody fool I had to come to America, like a bloody fool I had to come to America... I...had...to...come...to

129

He stops me, he takes the rifle away with his good hand.

"But it's *him*," I yell. "The one gave me those pictures, and now you can see how they shot him, he's lying down there, and two of them trying to go through his pockets. So while they're within range, why not..."

"Never mind," Everett says. He keeps that barrel pointed away. "Get down behind that window," he says.

Both of us crouch down again behind the blinds. And not a second soon enough. Because bullets splatter against the boards again, the first time in hours they fired this way.

"Nothing we could do anyway," he says to me. "And with only our few bullets left, we can't waste 'em. But that shows they haven't gone anywhere, they're still there . Still fixin' to come up and get us."

"He was young too, blonde he was. Shoved those drawings right into my hand. I can't remember the name he told... Rogers, Ridgdale, something like that... do you have any idea?"

"No," Everett says. And sits silent, crouched on the floor. Not three feet away in the middle of the room is that crazy contraption he made, that pipe planted in dirt, like an iron tree stump. My arms are aching from all the buckets of dirt I carried up for it. But now it's getting late afternoon, the sun's going down by the ridge.

"Do you think Albie's got to the road by now?"

"If everything went okay..."

"But you said it's only a few min..."

"I told you already, Ma'am. Isn't no use goin' over it and goin' over it."

"Oh I hope he got to where someone'll come for help. If he only..."

"Alright, Ma'am. Let's not talk about it for a while," Everett says.

Sitting there by the light of the sun going down, his face is squinted with pain or sleep, I don't know which. But whatever happens, no one'll believe me anyway. Back home, sitting on their rocking chairs, no one'll ever believe that little Amy Williams who married that traveling doctor for teeth could ever have got into such a...

Hello. He must have dozed again. Talking in his sleep now, and this room too small for me to go anywhere not to hear.

"Julia," he cries. And sighs, sort of. "No, not in that condition, I can take care of it," he says. "What do you think you're doing in this field, get out of here!... Julia, Julia..."

"Wake up, Mr. Everett. Wake up!"

"Julia, Julia..."

"You're having a nightmare or something. Wake up..."

"*What?*" he says. And comes to with a blink. Looks at me for a minute. Don't seem like he knows who I am. And then he moves, shakes his head.

"Shall I change that bandage again?"

"What?"

"That bandage. Looks like I'll have to change it again. Because it's soaking red some more..."

"Bandage," he says, "bandage?"

The poor man. He don't even hear me. Dreaming of her, thinking of *her*. And all around him, this room and the others, what she left must be paining the soul of the man. All alone like this, and that dead woman's traces all around...

Oh I wish Albie'd come back! He must have found something going by on that road by now. Because if he has to walk in the dark all that way, if he isn't got through to Buffalo yet...

The woman stares at me and the man too. Then they look at each other. That horse of theirs keeps whinnying, kicking back at the buckboard.

"Easy boy," the man says. "You don't want to drink too fast. All that water's got to have some place to go to..."

"You leave him alone, Charlie," the woman says. "Let that poor boy drink up all he wants."

"Please Ma'am," I say. "If you could only please take me to Buffalo. Because my Ma is left in that house and they said the sheriff would..."

"Wait a minute, boy. Hold on," says the man. "Can't you see what direction this wagon's headed? We gotta make Claremont by tomorrow morning, because..."

"Please, please. She wrote it in the note, she said that..."

"Note? What note are you talking about, boy?"

"Give it here, boy," the man says, and I hand it to him. My feet are aching, and that water's sloshing all around inside me. But then that woman says, "Why what's the matter boy. Take off your shoes."

"Please Ma'am. If you could only drive me to Buffalo..."

"Look at that, Charlie! The boy's feet are all bruised, he must have come miles this way... You take those stockings off right away, boy."

"Listen to this," says the man. And then he reads the note Ma wrote. They keep questioning me. But all the while it's getting darker, and we're not moving at all.

"Charlie, turn this buckboard around!."

"But I gotta get to that auction in Claremont tomorrow, so why not take him with us there, and..."

"Can't you read what's written down? People being killed in their very homes, murdered for all we know, and this poor boy here come all this way on foot..."

"But sheriff Angus'll know what to do, and..."

"Did you hear me," that woman shouts. "You turn this rig around. You know as well as I it's more'n twice as far to Claremont..."

"But Marian..."

"I'm not asking your opinion," she shouts. "Turn this rig around!"

"Please Sir, if you could just take me to Buffalo..."

"He's going to do it," the woman says. "Now don't you worry, boy. Charles!" she yells once more, turning to the man.

"All those horses, we're not going to have another chance to pick up one that cheap," he grumbles. But he does it just the same. Turns the buckboard around. And off we go, galloping towards Buffalo.

RIDGLEY

It just shows you what fear'll do. Just for money alone, nothin' and no man probably could have got this miserable group of heroes to finish the job I promised to do here. But when they hear how they won't be safe, when it's told how they need to protect themselves, and get animals to ride away on besides – look at them rushing to obey orders.

It's the secret of Command!. Why I could have probably been somebody famous, a General, a legend among the troops. If only I hadn't thrown it away on what those doctors said. But this makes up for it. Because I wouldn't be surprised, in fact, if we were actually outnumbered right now – with all the fire they sent down before and no sign of capitulation... Oh but when my men get that wagon pushed up in place way up on top of that other ridge like I ordered, when they set fire to that piled straw, and send the whole thing crashing down, we'll see what happens. Because it's only a few hundred yards up, how can they miss? That wooden house will go up like kindling. And then with me and those other two waiting for the smoke to flush them out just like rabbits beat out of the brush, – oh it'll be a real slaughtering victory.

But I have to keep my mind off sleep. Mustn't think about it. Concentrate on *details*, that's it. *Will power*, a man's strong as his own will!.. All these others, if I'd a let them, they'd 've bolted long ago! Sure, what's holding them here? – Only my own *will*, loyalty to the mission! So as long as I can keep awake, and it'll be all over soon now. There they go, half way up the back side of that hill. Forty minutes to go, I hope I gave them enough time to reach the top. Oh but my eyes feel like gravel was poured into them. If I could talk to someone, If I could just stop thinking about it – but there's only Ramos and Baring and that miserable Blanding down here. I'll just have to sit and wait. The mission, think of the mission! That's it. I'm not sleepy, I'm not sleepy. Have to keep telling myself, I'm not tired, not sleepy at all...

HOOK

He agreed! Ramos finally agreed to do it! So that's settled. Now we got him!, - all we have to do is wait a while!

Every single one of us has had some sleeping, except that murderin *Generalissimo*! And he isn't gonna be able to hold out much longer, his face is awful. So when that burning load of straw smashes into that house, I figure we'll have about three minutes to do what we gotta do. Rush Ridgley, grab that money sack of his, jump on those horses.

It won't be long! You goddamn murdering make-believe General, with three of us waiting to jump you, it won't be long! Look at his eyes, he probably couldn't even hit one of us at this range now, if he wanted I. But go ahead, you butchering loco head! Count the minutes, watch them on the hill, struggling with their burning load of hay.

It won't be long.

COREY EVERETT

"Quick, Ma'am. Wake up, you gotta help me..."

"Why..." she says. "Has Albie come back?"

"Over there. Look, on that hill..."

"Where? Oh it's a fire. But I didn't mean to fall asleep. How long have I..."

"Never mind now! Quick, my whole right arm's numb from the shoulder down, we got to get this pipe and box over to the north window!"

"But what is it, who are they? What's makin' that fire?"

"Going to try to fire us out of here, Ma'am. It's a wagon burning hay, or maybe wheat, and they've been pushing it up that ridge. But it was so dark at first, I couldn't see anything till they lit that flame."

"Where's my rifle, I must've put it ..."

"No use looking for it, Ma'am. We haven't got but half a dozen rounds left, and wouldn't do no use shooting up there, you couldn't see where to shoot, least ways hit anything..."

"But are we..."

"This contraption, Ma'am. Now's the time to see if any good's left in those old shells I found. Here, help me push the box over..."

"I.. I can't move it..."

"We've got to move it, Ma'am. Come on, try once more. *Push!*. That's it. Keep pushing hard."

That old box full of dirt doesn't hardly budge at first. Then it gives !. It trails dirt all over the place, and that pipe clanging, and me carrying one of those three rusty shells. Only she decides to have a spell of nerves.

138

"Albie... Albie..."

"Cut that out. CUT THAT OUT!"

What with that fire flaring like hell's fire on top of the north hill. And all the strain she's been under, she starts trembling and moaning. I have to slap her once, smart across the face. Then she looks at me. Stiffens.

"Take this shell in your hands, Ma'am. Hold it like this... QUICK. TAKE IT."

I kneel down. Weakness, nausea, a hot fever comes riddling through me. For a second all I see is her knees, trembling through that worn cotton skirt. My head goes around. But then I manage to shake it off, biting till blood's drawn from one lip.

I can't even aim this crazy thing, don't even know where the damn shell'll go. It might even explode right here in this room, kill us outright, save them the trouble. But anyways, what else have we got to try? Our food most gone, our water pails most empty, no sign of that boy for hours now, and Buffalo too many miles away to expect strangers. Her and me in this one room, and only these three old shells left. So we got to try it. Even if it don't do nothing but scare them for a while, it might be long enough so that maybe if that boy got through, if those Buffalo people, by some chance are riding this way...

"I see them, I see them!," the woman's yelling. "Look, two or three around that wagon away up there and pushing it into the edge of the cliff so..."

"Allright, now, Ma'am. When I say drop, you just drop that shell with that end first right smart in that open end of this pipe, and then get down the hell out of the way, get right down on the floor."

"It's heavy, I don't know if I can..."

"That's alright, Ma'am. Hold it up high now, right over the end. Now I'm going to try to move this pipe a little – there she is. Alright. You ready?"

She holds that ancient shell over that rusted pipe. I'm meanwhile maneuvering it with my good arm, trying to keep it aimed. Then suddenly calmness comes back into her eyes. She looks at me. For a few seconds we stay like that, staring at each other, and waiting.

ALBIE FINLETTER

"Go ahead boy," the sheriff says to me, and hoists me up on the table. "Now tell all about it..."

"Well, my ma and me were comin' from Alberton, and got lost, and..."

140

"Don't be afraid, boy. Like you told it to us on the way," says the woman.

And the man she calls Charles goes on.

"Everyone here wants to help you, boy."

But what are they standing around for, why doesn't somebody do something?. It's a saloon, that's what it is!. And all these men standing around me, all lined up on the bar. I can feel their eyes boring into me too, though it isn't unkindness, it's more sort of a questioning look, sort of like they're all waiting to hear if I'm lyin or not..'.

"We were all comin' from Illinois, and got lost, and..."

Then I tell them!. I tell them the whole thing, everything that's happened. More and more people crowding into the place, some women too, and after I stop there isn't a face smiling anywhere. Then a woman, ~I don't know who she is,~ walks up to that Sheriff, Manning his name is, and cries out in a loud voice.

"What are you standing there for, Jim? You heard the boy!
. So if Corey Everett's going to be upheld..."

"By God," a voice yells. "Deputies is what you need!"

"A posse!"

"Deputize us, deputize us!"

Then the whole place goes crazy. Not wild or anything like that, I mean nobody's screaming or yelling or busting things, but men are rushing around, buttoning on coats and guns, and that Sheriff Manning, the one I was took to with my note, he gets up on the table where I am and he starts talking.

"Bill MacDonald's to take the section north of Hollingshead meadow!. Round everyone up!... I don't care whether they're propagating the race or not, you rustle them up in front of Loren's barber shop. And Ike Brandley's to take the area south of Hollingshead. I'll go down Main Street myself with the boy, and I want every man able to ride to meet us in front of Loren's for the deputizing. Alright, let's go," he yells, and everyone rushes out into the street.

What a crazy fast ride! Me on the saddle in front of that Sheriff Manning, both of us tearing up and down the main street of Buffalo, and him shooting his gun into the air, and yelling at closed windows.

"Corey Everett's being ambushed, they got him besieged, it's hired riders are doing it! So we're deputizing in the square in front of Loren's barber shop in ten minutes! No one's excepted, less he's too sick to care about his own lawful rights in Fargos county!"

And then off we jump to another place, and then another, and pretty soon the whole main street is jingling and teaming with people, and still we aint left Buffalo, and Ma and him're still all alone up there in that shot up house. But when there isn't an empty space around and me are sitting with angry looks on horses all around, the sheriff, he asks someone to get a blanket for me. And after they bring it, he steps out on the porch of that barber shop.

"Everybody's right hand high," he says, and everyone waiting puts his hand in the air.

"I'm deputizing you,: the Sheriff yells, "Because we're going to decide once and for all who makes the law and who doesn't in Fargos County!. When it's lawful for a man to stake out a claim according to the Government, and breed what he wants on it, it's lawful for his friends to see that no one bothers him in doin' it. You all know the trouble we've been having for a long time from certain tin horn ranchers around here, and everyone sitting here knows I never once said we ought to declare war back on 'em, because isn't nothing' ever comes out of that but more feuding."

"But orneriness is one thing, and murder is another!. And I'm telling every man here that we aim to get whoever's behind this ruckus at Everett's place, and set up our own protection so isn't nothing' like that's going to happen again

143

in our County!. It's us who make the laws and it's us has a stake in seein' they're carried out, and that don't mean that a man's gotta have three hundred head before he's protected! So what I want's your promise to defend the laws of this county and State, and obey me in carrying out my rightful orders!"

Such a yell! The shutters right near where I'm sitting begin to rattle, and guns go off like it was the fourth of July. Then the sheriff turns to me, and all those raised hands go down.

"Alright boy," he says. "You lead us..." We head South out of town.

FINALE

It nearly frightens us out of our wits! A loud whoosh, and then an explosion from a regular shell or something not twenty yards from that burning wagon on the hill. Rocks and dirt go careening up and we can hear them yelling from up there, some of them must have been hit. I don't know why they aint never used that piece before if they had it all this while. But that decides Ramos' mind quick just in case anything was holding him back. So now me and Ramos and Baring make our move, rushing up at Ridgley before he knows what's happening, because that explosion made him jump too, standing slack-jawed, and both his guns down.

He had only time for just one shot before we get to him, Ramos and me pummeling him and smashing him down. Only Baring isn't with us. He's lying not five feet away, that one bullet got him. But that means there's only two of us now to split whatever's left.

"Never mind!" Ramos is yelling at me. "The horses. We gotta get out of here. If they turn that crazy cannon on us..."

But I aint done yet.

"Crazy play-acting butcher!" I can't seem to stop myself, kicking that high and mighty, spitting down at him.

146

"Without them two fancy pistols, what's happened to your high and mighty act? Goddamn miserable play-acting..."

"Come on!" Ramos is pulling at me. "Never mind!. We gotta get on the horses."

"Leave him here, after what he done?"

"It's our own skins, come on."

"In a second. Here, help me."

I don't want to shoot him, not yet. Let them take it out of his hide, and blow him to pieces with that cannon of theirs! But I want it to be slow, in stages, and without him being able to do nothing but yell back. So Ramos and me tie the little Napoleon to that bragging flag of his and stick it in the ground right where they can't help hitting him if they try at all. He still isn't come to, but he isn't dead by a long shot, though that hook gashed his face. Oh I'd like to take it and push it against his throat and...

"Never mind for Chris' sakes!" Ramos is yelling. "Come on!."

All the gold the skunk had on him we put in our own pockets, and I stick something else in my shirt besides: it's that fancy belt belonging to that dead Colonel, full of red and gold stones, maybe rubies for all I know, and Ramos never seen me do it. I got those two gold revolvers too.

"Are you coming?"

"Okay, here, help me up.."

Then we're riding away from that pig thole of a place, leaving those others on the hill with that burning wagon of theirs, McKensie and Williams and Donaldson. But the hell with them, it isn't our fault they picked to do like Ridgley said! Then we hear another whoosh, and a terrible boom, and looking back we see something godawful!

A great flash where that shell hits high above where that burning wagon is, and a rattling rumbling roar, like boulders loose. Everything starts rushing down. That wagon goes smash right over the side, sparks and fire flying in a perfect arc and falling with a crash, and that noise getting bigger in a wild landslide of rocks, and every once in a while screaming and yells, because they must have got trapped right in front, it must have buried every one of them up there, and that huge ugly roar echoing on, and pieces of that burning wagon glowing in the darkness, scattered to hell and gone!

"What's the matter with you?" Ramos is pullin' at me grabbing the bridle. "You can't go back there."

"If that house was buried with all those rocks, if there's no one left to kill the little Napoleon..."

"Never mind, the hell with him! We gotta make Claremont, and with no water, with these horses fevered up as it is...."

He takes the bridle and leads it away, and we head off into the dark. No path to see yet, but when it's light we'll find the Claremont road, and from Claremont there's stages leaving for the Southwest every nightfall. So all we got to do is wait till it gets a little light, and be rid of this hellish business once and for all! But oh if I ever leave Dallas again, I'll be hog-tied and roped, or laid in a box, or let them shoot me first, so help me God!

In a few minutes it's all behind us. We can't even hear that rumbling any more. But looking across that dark black, we can still see fires burning.

MRS. AMY FINLETTER

The first thing I notice is the sky: pasty and pale, the color of some kind of cheese, like just before sunrise. Then I notice a sound: like a man yelling, or reciting, or something dim and far away, coming from far off, like through tree branches or water. Then I begin to recollect. My eyes begin to focus. I see that pipe twisted and dirt blown all around,

149

and pieces of that third shell where it hit against the ceiling, exploding and almost killing both of us, Corey and myself, as we lay on the floor.

He still isn't opening his eyes, but I manage to get to him. Everything aches, but I can move alright. And after some of that plastery water's splashed in his eyes, he stirs a little, wakes up, looks at me for a minute without knowing who I am.

"Are you allright?"

"Julia..."

"No, it's Amy Finletter. We must have both been lying here for a a spell because—"

"Amy Finletter?"

Then he tries to sit up. I pour the last water over him. But luckily that shot shoulder wasn't the one he'd been layin on...

"Where are they, what's that noise?"

"I've only lost my senses for a few seconds. But I don't think that..."

"Listen," he says.

"Who's that shouting?"

We both wade through the pile of debris inside that shattered room, and get to a window. My God, you never seen such a sight! Rocks, hundreds of 'em, boulders and smaller ones, ~ all piled up on the south side of the place, and all the way down the hill and in the fields south of us, ~ pieces of that wagon still smoking. But no one's about, though we can still hear a crazy hoarse yelling somewhere... And outside of that, a strange stillness.

"Why," he says. "it's that second shot done it, before I lost my balance and almost killed us shooting off our own roof!. That second shot, pure fool's luck!. Because look how near that wagon came, talk about *close*! Well, all those men on the hill had to've been buried probably~"

"Listen," I tell him.

It's a crazy sound. Yelling, or more like ranting, and eerie in these surrounds. But we can't make out any words at this distance, though it's coming from down below. Then he says for me to take his rifle and divides the bullets, all we have left.

"Where are you going? You can't mean to go down there..."

"I've got a hunch, Ma'am. You cover me..."

"Leave me alone up here? With them ready to..."

"Isn't nobody left down there Ma'am, according to what my hunch says. So if you'll cover me..."

"If you think I'm going to stay alone up here..."

151

But he pushes open that splintered door, begins trotting down the path, his rifle dangling from his good arm. Silence all around, the heat's beginning to come up again, that crazy yelling rising from down in the valley. I watch him go.

Then my mind gives a flick, and something else comes back to me with a shock: Albie.

COREY EVERETT

"A Court Martial offense! Do you hear that, Blanding? A Court Martial offense! Hanging or the firing squad, take your pick, I don't care! But there' no other way, mutiny is mutiny under the law. Your actions force me, Blanding, to..."

It's a man yelling! Tied to a flag he is, and both eyes staring like a crazy man's, and his mouth jerking with little snake movements, and scratches all over him, and a big gash on his face. Something familiar in his face too, but I can't place him. And wearing what looks like part officers clothes from the Civil War, a Confederate hat and belt, and shouting wild as if I weren't even around.

"Yes Sir, I'll have to give my evidence then. But make it quick as possible, I don't care for these trials. Because you understand, Sir, anything in the nature of testimony like this is repugnant to my calling as an officer, though you may think it' strange, Sir but to be separated from my troops even so much as for a few days is – if I do say so, Sir – extremely hard. Because they've shown me a loyalty that is far beyond the usual..."

He don't even notice me! But what happened here, who shot these others? This place looks like it was hit by a tornado. No horses either, nothing, no one else around. Hello, here's something, looks like graves, fresh dug. And a well, they dug themselves a well. And here's the one she talked about, that gave her those sketches which...

"You Sir. I demand to be taken to the Commanding Officer, I will surrender only to rank worthy of accepting my sword, and I suggest only for the sake of alleviating further bloodshed..."

Yelling at me? Yes, he's looking straight at me, talking away. But look at those dead sheep scattered all over, and my fields, scorched and pulled up, and everything, oh all these months of work pilloried by a goddamn lawless bunch of...

"Military Courtesy!. I stand on my rights under Military Courtesy! . I have the option to review your victorious troops, Sir! Yes, and surrender this flag in proper ceremony..."

Out of his head, plumb out of his head!. But still I ought to take this gun and blow his brains out, because after what they've done here, and all those weeks of lost work...

"I demand Sir! On my rights as defeated commander, to review the garrison before yielding up my sword..."

No I can't shoot him. Even if he's loco now, he's the one can tell most about what happened if they ever get him talking straight. So I untie his feet, sweating, because it isn't easy, my right hand's numb and I have to cut the cord. But all the way up the hill through that pile of twisted stones and burned pieces, and bodies, me in back with my rifle pointed at his neck, and him marching in front with that flag still tied to where his hands are bound in back, he keeps on talking away.

"A brilliant strategy, Captain. Oh yes, I don't mind saying it, I give credit where credit's due! Because we had every advantage except in terrain, yes, and if it weren't for the rankest kind of treachery, which in all my years of campaigning I have never seen equaled, I think we still might have given you a fight."

On and on and on. But when I push him inside our wrecked stinking room, and she gets a good look at him, she gives a cry.

154

"It's *him*!. He put the blindfold on me. He's the one that questioned me, that made me put the cloth over my eyes!."

But the madman doesn't even recognize her.

"Where's the troops?" he's shouting. Looking this way and that, nudging into every corner, whipping himself around to start at me. "I demand Sir, as a matter of Military Courtesy..."

"There isn't no troops!. Take a look. All there is this woman and me!."

"What! No, you can't lie to me Sir! Grenades and an artillery piece were in this garrison, my men made several assaults in waves."

"There isn't no garrison!. Do you understand? There isn't no troops, there isn't no garrison, there isn't no artillery!. No grenades, no nothing at all. Just this woman and me."

"A lie! I demand to see the troops, on my rights as defeated Commander! Whatever Military Courtesy may be in force here, you can't refuse me the right to review the soldiers who..."

I finally have to take him into the bedroom and lock the door behind him. All the while he's still yelling, "Troops, troops, I ask to see the troops!"

"How much longer, Sheriff?"

"Steady boy. We're getting near now..."

"But why are we stopped, why are we losing time here when..."

"Only a minute or two, boy. We got to water our horses. Because this is a long ride and that heat's gonna be even worse than you seen before this day's out."

"But I don't want to wait, every minute with my Ma up there and Mr. Everett makes them liable to—

"Alright, steady boy!, We're going to take off right this minute. MacDonald, you take half the men and circle around by old Creek Road from the South, and we'll go in on the main road. Three quick shots is what I'll give if you're not to ride close in. You wait to hear... Allright, let's go!."

HOOK

"You and your sense of direction!" Ramos yells.

"But you said we shouldn't 've taken that other trail..."

"What do you mean *me*? Who was the one braggin' on how he could feel his way along."

"*I* braggin! When it was *me* dragged you out of there, made you quit in the first place?"

"Never mind. I'm getting tired of listening to you shoot your mouth off..."

I don't answer. No use telling a scared rabbit anything. Because that's why he's turning on me now, he's scared, too scared to think straight.

Look at those damn hills! Like rattlesnakes hide, and at the same time, full of marshy ground that got no call to be stuck in the middle of this wilderness. But I'm not saying we're lost. If we keep our heads, and as long as this trail leads us back to the Claremont road....

Oh, oh, oh. There goes my pack, smack on the ground, those old straps must have torn. But how am I going to fasten it on again, and that wrist of mine not much good for anything. He's got to help me.

"Ramos, Ramos..."

"Come on!. What's the matter with you?"

"My pack fell off. Here, I can't get it back on the saddle horn..."

"We're losing time..."

"It's you who are losing it, you Muckhead, jawing away when we could have had it back on the horse by now!."

As long as he's okay, what does he care? But I don't trust him as far as a snail can jump..

"Can't you hurry up with that?" he says, and comes over to lift it, and right there between us on the ground, something falls out. He picks it up. But he don't put it back. He just stands there and when I feel inside the pack I know what it is.

"Real perfect for imitation diamonds," I say, "but anyway I can use that belt for actual wearing, even though it wasn't intended for wear."

"*Imitation?*" Ramos yells. And turns facing me. "*Imitation!*"

"You don't think that Colonel'd ever spend what real stones'd cost, do you? And him a tin horn if we ever met up with one!."

"I think you're a goddam liar!" Ramos yells. "Trying to get away with this belt, and me with my pockets full of nothing but air.."

"I claimed it first, it's mine! Everybody heard me speak up for those two guns and that belt too, and isn't nobody going to tell me different."

158

"Slow down," says Ramos, backing from me. "Who you makin' speeches to…?"

I jump him before his finger touches the gun barrel! It has to be quick!. Can't let him get a chance to draw, and me with one wrist out of commission! So I use the hook hard, yelling and swearing. And when I come to, he's lying back and I'm trying to pull it out of him, and that belt's flung twenty yards away in a mighty heave he gave just before he fell.

I'm trembling all over, shaking so my legs won't stay still. Can't do anything about cleaning the hook either right now, just have to let it be. But imagine that dirty rotten half breed,~trying to blackguard me out of what's rightfully mine! No, you can't trust any of them! So three minutes is all it takes to empty his pockets, and then I go to get that belt.

I can see it plain, glittering in the sun, it's hanging from some kind of a scrub or bush the other side of a grassy stretch. But I haven't got time right now for detours. So running and stumbling I am, and set out across the patch of grass and all of a sudden my feet just start giving way. It's like as if there isn't no bottom at all, my legs start sinking, and I can't grab anything to hold on to except that oatmeal ground which I should've known was quicksand by the looks of it.

159

Over my waist already, I can't get freed. Screaming won't do no good, there aint nobody to hear except him , and he isn't helping nobody!. But someone's got to be nearby. Help, help... never mind the goddam belt, I don't want anything, the guns too, take everything, but just let me get out of this!... Please, help me somebody! Is that a sound... horses? Oh help me somebody help me somebody help...

"It's riders allright," Everett says. "We better get down out of view."

"But those men are gone. We've been everywhere, and..."

"I'm not sure they're not coming back, whatever's left of them. Because finding your way out of here isn't easy, and they might have got lost."

"I want to ride to Buffalo, you said we was going to Buffalo."

"So we are, Ma'am. I mean for us to. But now that we got bullets from that case down there, it won't do to get ambushed, will it? After we come through all we did?"

160

So both of us wait in that wrecked room. There's no noise behind us, he's stopped his wild yells. But all I can think of is where Albie is. Four days ago – was it only four days – the three of us come riding up this hill asking for a night's board, and in four days the whole world's changed. My Albie's grown, maybe lost, Finletter's dead, and this man next to me closer in some ways then kin can ever be. I don't know how we're going to take our leave of one another when the time comes. But then I hear him shouting.

"Down the gorge," he says, shaking me a little.

"Look..."

"As if I wouldn't ever *not* know that face! Yelling, and frantic, and seated astride the Sherrif's own horse, holding on tight with both hands, and whooping and hollering and laughing and crying, it seemed, all at once! Then those Buffalo men're crowding into the cabin, and one of them, the man I writ the note to, asking, 'Who done it, where'd they come from, what was it happened Corey?'"

"*Happened?*" he says, and grins suddenly at me, the first time I seen that man smile since I came here. "Oh we had quite a ruckus," he says. "But it's all took care of now. With the help of some friends," he tells them, and smiles at Albie.

"But where'd they come from, who *were* they?"

"I got something to show you, Sheriff," Corey says.

All the men follow and we crowd through and Albie unbolts the door to the bedroom. And the first thing we see is legs, dangling legs, shoulder high, and above them that madman, his mouth silent, blood coming out of his nose, and his neck twisted in a home-made noose. And do you know what he'd hung himself with?

Yes, that flag. His own red flag with the words *"Death To Rustlers!"* stitched in the center. It's swinging his purple face from north to south in the breeze from the open cabin door.

EPILOGUE

Real cold out this morning, these Fall days are really nippy. But now that I got all my hay in, I don't care, let it snow when it wants. Anyway, I don't feel much like working today. Just lazing around, and waiting for them to finish their lessons up in the house. Amy's a real bear when it comes to his lessons," But, as she says, how's he going to learn more when it's only her teaching him? Anyway, what she'd like to do is send Albie clear off to Buffalo, board him for the winter months. But she knows we can't do that,– needing him on the place like we do. But she's a bear about some things. Clean feet in the house, for example. Soon shoot us as have us track dirt over that kitchen. Oh Albie and me, we got our troubles.

But right now I can't help thinking about everything that's happened these past months, because today's the fourteenth and that makes it just five months since they come riding up that hill in their wagon. All those terrible days, and then the trial of the Rutherford clan that come after, and how one old man had a stroke right in the middle of it, paralyzed so he can't talk, and him spending the rest of his time in that hospital in Fairfax. But with all that stuff they writ up in that papers, and all the publicity we

164

got, you'd have thought Arizona was New York for a couple of days. That weren't so important though as what everyone done later: coming out here, taking turns working, all the neighbors around, and some from as far as Buffalo. Was only three, four weeks, they had my place looking like it could be made decent again. Well, I aint never gonna forget that. Some things, it don't do no use to talk about them.

Still, maybe it's like them newspapers said, the whole county isn't ever going to forget what happened. Because look at the elections – first time in all these years we've changed over – and as for all those friends of the Squire's, nothing but silence and sweetness all the while from Buffalo to Claremont. Well, if they was aiming to accomplish something, it sure come to pass different from what they expected. More settlers coming into Fargos this past summer than the past two put together and the same thing's true for Claremont, Fairfax, all the rest.

Must be twenty thousand people living around Buffalo now... And those new roads they got started, and Bills for protecting our water rights, – oh I guess things isn't turned out like some people was hoping.

But what I'm wondering about is how long's Amy going to keep on going the way she is? I'm not unappreciative, I know how she's made the whole house over inside. But it's her strength I'm thinking of. Because we still don't have a doctor within thirty miles, and if she keeps insisting on helping the two of us outside, she might bring on a misfortune, lose the child that's coming. I have to put my foot down. I want that child as much as she, and just because she's so interested in making the place into...

"Hello. There's a wagon coming along the new creek road down there. Homesteaders if I ever saw them. Turning in at the hill, probably want watering. Look at the load they got, those poor animals are going to do a lot of suffering before they strike landfall."

"Pa, Pa, I'm finished, Pa."

"Albie, you quit running like that. If you tear those britches again..."

"Who's that coming up the hill, Pa?"

The boy's out of breath, but his Ma's following behind, so that means she isn't out of pleasure with him, the lesson must have been good. She isn't ever interested in talking to him if he isn't been apt. And here come those homesteaders now up to where I'm waiting for them, my well already primed and my greeting smile ready.

"Can I borrow your shotgun this evening, Pa?"

166

"Alright, Albie, we'll talk on it afterwards. Because it looks like we got guests coming right now."

The three of us wait by that well and when that wagon creeps to a halt, and that inquiring driver gets down, fatigued and dusty from riding, and his wife and two boys sitting there, watching him, I hold out my hand.

"Corey Everett's the name," I tell him. "My wife Amy, my boy Albie."

"Peter Branely from Pennsylvania."

"Looks like you could use some water from the looks of it..."

"I'd be mighty obliged," he says. And then gives a long look at my place after he's sipped, taking it all in, fields, stock, buildings, everything. And then sort of sighs.

"About three hundred acres," he guesses.

"Three hundred and twenty."

"Been here long?"

"About two years," I tell him.

He looks and looks. And then asks if they might not rest a while after riding all day, his wife and two boys clambering down from that groaning wagon. "And I'd count it a favor if you'd show me the place," he asks, but smiling with sort of shyness, as if he was afraid somebody might take offence.

167

"I'll do it, Pa, can I do it?" Albie asks.

I don't see no reason to object. So off they all go with Albie as guide, leaving Amy and me by the well beside their traveling household. And she's got her fingers in mine, smiling at me, as we hear that boy's voice raised across the field down below, shouting with pride and love and welling up clear as a bell.

"That's it, Mister!. As far as that road on the west side, and clear up to that new bunch of wire fence which my Pa just put in himself. And down as far as the road over to the south, and beyond the clover field. That's it. That's all our own land..."

AFTERWORD

For those interested, a film made from
"Incident in Fargos County" in 1954 – starring Dan Dureyea
and Kennan Wynn, & directed by Gerald Mayer at MGM –
called *"The Marauders"*, is available in DVD from
www. robertsvideos.com, tel 1-306-955-3763

Also available is the DVD version of
"The Ox Bow Incident" which can be purchased from www.
amazon.com starring Anthony Quinn, Mary Beth Hughes
and Dana Andrews, and directed by William Wellman in
1943.

www.ingramcontent.com/pod-product-compliance
Lightning Source LLC
Chambersburg PA
CBHW021102130626
46554CB00002B/482